P.S. I LOVE YOU

That night I wrote in my notebook: "*When we stand together, my head just comes up to his shoulders. He has nice hands. When he helped me climb his rock, he held his hand out to me and I took it. It felt warm and strong and I had the funny feeling that as long as I held onto his hand, I would never fall.*"

Bantam Sweet Dreams Romances
Ask your bookseller for the books you have missed

P.S. I LOVE YOU by Barbara Conklin
LITTLE SISTER by Yvonne Greene
LAURIE'S SONG by Suzanne Rand
PRINCESS AMY by Melinda Pollowitz
CALIFORNIA GIRL by Janet Quin-Harkin
THE POPULARITY PLAN by Rosemary Vernon
GREEN EYES by Suzanne Rand
THE THOROUGHBRED by Joanna Campbell
COVER GIRL by Yvonne Greene
LOVE MATCH by Janet Quin-Harkin
THE PROBLEM WITH LOVE by Rosemary Vernon
NIGHT OF THE PROM by Debra Spector
THE SUMMER JENNY FELL IN LOVE by
    Barbara Conklin
DANCE OF LOVE by Jocelyn Saal
THINKING OF YOU by Jeanette Nobile
HOW DO YOU SAY GOODBYE by Margaret Burman
ASK ANNIE by Suzanne Rand
TEN-BOY SUMMER by Janet Quin-Harkin

P.S. I Love You

Barbara Conklin

BANTAM BOOKS
TORONTO · NEW YORK · LONDON · SYDNEY

RL 5, IL age 11 and up

P.S. I LOVE YOU

A Bantam Book/September 1981
Sweet Dreams is a Trademark of Bantam Books, Inc.

Cover photo by Pat Hill.

ISBN 0-553-20323-1

Published simultaneously in the United States and Canada

PRINTED IN THE UNITED STATES OF AMERICA

To:
Robert S. Conklin, my husband
Dr. Pat Kubis, my teacher
Barbara and Connie, who were first to
 really know Mariah

Foreword

In one corner of my room there stands a creamy white-topped vanity table, dressed in yellow and white ruffles of organdy. I made the skirt a long time ago, all by hand, long before my mother bought our sewing machine that does everything.

Attached to the vanity are three mirrors hinged together and when tipped a certain way, I can see three of myself from three different angles. For sixteen years, I've watched myself grow up in those mirrors and sometimes when I peer intently into them, I can swear I not only see the outside of me, but the inside as well; the soul of me that no one can see—but me.

The most important part of this little table is not the creamy whiteness of the smooth top, not the cascades of carefully handmade ruffles, not even the three revealing mirrors. It is the shiny yellow bumper sticker I have pasted to the top of the middle mirror. It reads, P.S. I Love You.

The city of Palm Springs is proud of that bumper sticker. You can see it on so many cars all over California. I remember how hard I fought against our trip to that city the summer I turned sixteen, and now I know if I hadn't gone, I would have never met Paul. I would have never experienced the exhilarating joy of knowing him, of loving him, the agonizing frustration of knowing how it would all end. . . .

Chapter 1

Amy Iverson waited impatiently for me on the school steps, her long, dark hair hanging like dirty mop strings around her flushed round face. Her glasses were already steamed up because she was breathing so hard. She was clutching a long, narrow brown envelope in her sweaty fist and waving wildly at me.

It was one of those rare, terribly hot humid days in Laguna Beach, with hardly a breeze from the ocean. Just looking at my best friend made me wilt. I felt like jumping into the water that very second.

"We did it!" she shouted at me as I ran down the bleached white cement stairs, taking them two at a time. "We're juniors—at last!"

"I thought it would never end," I told her, pushing my sticky, long brown hair off of my neck. Grabbing as much of it as I could with my one free hand, I pulled it away from my wet neck and flapped it in the air, trying to feel a little breeze.

"Thank goodness they let us out before lunch," I said, wiping my forehead with a clean tissue.

Just the thought of us being juniors at last, though, carried me down the rest of the

3

stairs. Maybe IT would happen now. I'd seen IT happen to other girls—girls whom I didn't consider very attractive. It seemed to me that when the guys are aware that you are a junior, they become interested. There you are, going to the movies together, sharing the same beach towel, sipping date shakes in the little hut on the Pacific Coast Highway and then, finally, going to the prom in the spring!

It was a terrific time for me. I'd just turned sixteen last week. Now finally I was a junior and had the whole summer to look forward to. Plenty of time for me to do the one thing I most wanted to do for so long—write my own romantic novel and become famous by the time I was a senior.

I could see it all now. I would spend the summer writing out on my favorite rock by my ocean. By the time my junior year began, I would have the completed novel safely in the mail to some big publisher. Then, after waiting maybe a few weeks, I'd get this terrific contract and I'd be on my way! By the time I became a full-fledged senior, I'd have to literally fight off the offers of dates from boys, boys waiting in line to date a successful novelist.

Amy and I stopped on the bottom step and hugged each other, sweat and all. Then we raced down the grassy hill and headed for Talbot's meadows. It was a shortcut home, and we both were so terribly anxious to get on with it, to get the summer started!

"Are you really gonna write that book this summer, Mariah? Remember you were going to do it last summer and the summer before. . . ."

I pushed my face down into the tall yellow and green grass of the meadow and smiled. Just the delicious thought made happy chills quiver from my toes all the way up to my skinny fingers. I rolled over again and rested on the tip of my spine, propping myself up with my equally skinny elbows.

"Sure I am. And it's going to be really good," I promised Amy. "Just like Rosemary Rogers or Kathleen Woodiwiss or Denise Robins. Or maybe even like Fiona Harrowe. In fact, it'll be so great, maybe the publishers will think one of them really wrote it and is sending it in under a different name. And maybe, just maybe, they'll even want to make a movie out of it!"

Amy shot right up then, her chubby face glowing with anticipation, her dark brown eyes sparkling. "A movie," she moaned. "Oh, Mariah. . . ." But then her face wrinkled all up in a frown. "But when they find out that you're only sixteen—not even through high school yet—they might not even want to read it!"

I let out a heavy sigh of impatience and disgust for Amy's ignorance. "Oh, Amy! They won't know I'm sixteen." I flicked a lost ladybug off my jeans.

"But they have to find out sooner or later," Amy said, standing up and stretching. The orange-red ladybug landed on her arm and she jumped away in fright.

I laughed. "It's just a ladybug," I told her. "By the time they find out, the contract will be signed. Anyhow, when they do eventually find out, they'll be thrilled about it. I'll be their protégé as I climb the bestseller list!"

Amy just sighed as we walked toward home. I really didn't think she knew what a protégé was and I expected her to ask me, but she didn't. By the time we were in front of her house, a huge stone and brick structure with vibrant pink bougainvillea growing all over it, we were hotter than ever and all I could think of was the ocean.

I waved goodbye to Amy and headed for the highway. I hated crossing the busy thing, but I refused to walk all the way down to the crosswalk.

"Hey, wait," Amy called and I turned. She ran up close to me and smiled. She had removed her glasses for our run through the meadow and had now returned them to her rounded nose. She was peering through the thick lenses at me as though she was trying to read the sign across the street.

"I've read some of these romances, you know." She looked all around the field and started to whisper even though there was absolutely no one around. "Mariah, are you going to write the juicy parts, you know, the ladies with big heaving breasts?"

I kicked a gray stone off a grassy mound, and it flew to the centerline of the highway. "If the part calls for a big bosom, I'll have to, well, do some research, see how they handle it, you know...."

"And the love parts?" Amy went on seriously.

"I'll handle it," I told her with confidence. She smiled and we waved goodbye again, but as I ran across the highway, dodging the cars rounding the curve, my confidence was weakening. How would I handle it? Certainly not from experience.

Amy and I were both extremely shy. Maybe that's what drew her to me in the first place; we both seemed to need each other in a funny way. Her problem had always been her weight. She wasn't terribly fat, at least I didn't think so, but when you're our age, having any amount of excess weight was a big problem. Still, Amy had done her very best to get the boys to notice her and ask her out—even for just a ride on the back of their mopeds, or maybe their cars if they had one. She had tried setting the dark, thick strands of hair so many times, but by noon, the strands turned into strings and she would usually just give up and shove it all into a rubber band and let it hang at the back of her neck. Nothing she did seemed to work.

My trouble was a little different. I couldn't smile. I mean, I just don't have a face that smiles easily in front of boys. I can be laughing, really hysterical with a bunch of girls, but when a boy walks into the room I can feel my whole body tense up, my face go from a pleasant happy, oval shape into a perfect nerd of a square. I can actually feel my lips form steel wedges and realize that's just how the boys see me.

Adults think I'm very serious, too. But they always say how pretty I am, especially my dark eyes. Actually I sort of like looking "deep and mysterious," but the kids probably think I look sad and gloomy. No doubt the boys do.

I also have my nose in a book most of the time. I'm sure most of the more interesting guys think I'm not interested in them in the slightest way. I've been told I even look bored.

My grades come easily to me, but I have a terrible urge to read everything and anything I can get my hands on. For two years now I have thought of nothing but to turn out my own romantic novel and become famous. Maybe then some boy will take a closer look.

Amy has to really study to get good grades, but in one way she's not stupid. She is just as aware as I am that life is passing us by without one of us being asked out on a date. How will I ever be able to write about a big romance if I've never had one?

Ever since I was fourteen I'd put off writing, waiting for that real romance to happen. But I would wait no longer. This was it, this was the summer I would finally write—romance or no romance!

"My imagination will just have to do," I said aloud. I looked down now at the stone in the middle of the highway and kicked it the rest of the way across.

My feet practically flew down the path, the one I had beaten down with my feet ever since I'd started school. I parted the oleander bushes and squeezed through. The salty, tangy smell of my ocean greeted me, filling my head with a tingling sensation of being home.

Our house sits on the top of a rocky, steep

hill and from just about any room you can look down and see the ocean, swelling in and out in a never-ending dance. Looking further down the strip of sand, you can see the city of Laguna Beach. In the daylight you can spot hundreds of homes dotting the cliffs and hills. Some of them are Spanish, some are Old English, and some are rustic cottages whose windows and patios turn toward the sea. Intermingled with them are motels and hotels and restaurants, and unique little shops that display the work of local artists. At night the coastline becomes a black, soft strip of velvet, with tiny jewels of lights displayed on its softness. I never get tired of staring at this view.

As soon as I scurried through the front door I headed straight to my room. I practically tore off my sweaty clothes and changed into my favorite yellow bandeau. Then I headed for the beach.

The sea gulls scurried around when I took over their perch, a large rock, looking over the waves. It was as if they were mumbling and grumbling since they all had to reposition themselves. I'd been scrambling up on that rock all of my life, and why they still didn't trust me I didn't know. Maybe they were just different sea gulls.

"You all look alike to me," I hollered at them. Did people all look alike to them, I wondered.

The rock was a good place to think, and I had a lot to think about. I assumed most romance writers lived in really neat places, pretty surroundings where they think their books out. Well, at least I was ahead of the game on that one.

Amy and I had been friends for a long time, ever since I could remember, but there are things I don't even tell her. Or anyone. Like how it was when my father walked out, and how many rejection slips I'd received from magazines where I'd submitted my short stories. I'd written poems, too, but no one seemed to like them either.

Anyhow, I'd already come to the conclusion that poems and short stories are just not my thing. After reading a few romantic novels, it occurred to me that perhaps I'd have better luck in that category. The romances are great and they're sold everywhere, even in supermarkets, so I began to pick some up about a year ago while doing some innocent shopping for my mother. Now that I have my own driver's license, I do it quite often.

The novels are usually very fat paperbacks— you really get your money's worth in reading— and they have terrific, passionate covers. My closet was so crammed full of the books, there was absolutely no place anymore for my shoes.

I had my novel all figured out and outlined in one of my shorthand notebooks. On the first page I'd written: "Exotic Place." The background for the book can't just be anywhere—it must be in a place that sounds mysterious, enticing, exciting, and somewhere far off where the reader probably has never been so that you can kind of skirt around the details (and bluff a little).

Then you have to have a girl, a heroine with a gorgeous figure. She must be really innocent and untouched. That is extremely important because when she is finally not innocent anymore and finally touched, the reader has got to be there and go through it with her.

Then you have to have her living under terrible conditions, like a bad stepfather or something and so she escapes it all, or tries to. But the tragedy comes when she gets into even more trouble and then THE MAN always enters.

He's got to be really good-looking, in a gruff sort of fashion. I would choose mine to have very dark curly hair and his muscles would have muscles. I sighed at the delicious thought that I could make him absolutely anything I wanted to.

Most of the stories take place centuries ago, but I could research that part. After I completed the book (it would be an instant success, of course, and they would ask for more), I would have loads of money—money that would solve all my problems.

First there is my mother. Her greatest passion is reading the travel folders she picks up at an agency down in Laguna Beach. She leaves them all over the house. She also cuts out the travel section of the *Los Angeles Times* every Sunday.

If I had the money, I'd buy her plane trips to wherever she wanted to go. Time off from her work would be no problem because she wouldn't have to work another day in her life. I would buy her new clothes, too. She goes to that day school where she teaches in the same things every day. Not that she doesn't look nice. I've often just stood back and tried to view my mother with a stranger's eyes so that I could get an impartial opinion, and I always come up with the final conclusion that my mother is strikingly beautiful. With new clothes, I felt she'd be a knockout.

Her hair is the color of a caramel candy, still in its shiny, see-through wrapper. It bounces like the hair on the girls on the television shampoo commercial so, I bet if you put your nose in it, it would smell like a shop full of beautifully scented candles.

Her eyes are an honest brown, not like mine. Mine look like they are cheating because they have little green and yellow specks in them—I think people call that hazel. But my mother's are a true, true brown, and they always smile with her face. She doesn't have a freckle on her body, so I guess I got mine from my father. She never, never gets pimples on her chin like I sometimes do, unless she overdoses on chocolate. I can't remember her ever saying the word "diet" because she's never had to.

Money could change her whole life. And maybe, just maybe, one of her trips could be to Chicago to bring my father back home.

Then there is Kim, my sister, who's just six years old. Sometimes she's a doll, and sometimes she can be a real brat. But I find I usually love her no matter which role she's playing. Her hair is a bright orange-red, and she hates it. Her body came with its own set of freckles that you wouldn't believe, but my mother says that a lot of them will fade with age. That's terribly important to Kim because she wants to be a dancer when she grows up. She attends beginner's dancing lessons twice a week after school.

With the money from my first book, I figured I could send her to a better school, a private one, and maybe send her to one in Paris or Russia when she is older. My mother could then say, "Yes, I have two daughters, one a famous writer and one a famous dancer with the Paris Ballet. . . ."

I wouldn't have minded having Kim's red hair so long as it was curly like hers. Mine is a mousy (and a dead mouse at that) brown color and is so straight you can almost hear it cry out when I try to bend it around a roller.

That's probably what I like best about writing. No one needs to know what you look like when they read your work.

Well, I thought, looking around me, watching the sea gulls line up on the beach, I don't have a bestseller yet. I don't even have a typewriter, but I do have this summer. I'll start this afternoon. I flipped the pages of my shorthand book and waited for the inspiration that was bound to come and start it all.

Chapter 2

My feet felt hot and itchy, so I pulled off my sandals and used the jagged, black rocks for a foot scratcher. The sea gulls finally settled down again, probably deciding I could be trusted. Our white clapboard house with blue shutters at the windows stared back down at me from its precarious perch on the hill. I could see the yellow and white organdy curtains stirring a little in my bedroom window on the second floor. That was one great thing about my bedroom—there's always a breeze. The other great thing is that the view from the window right above my desk is fantastic.

I'd bought that desk in a secondhand store in Santa Ana three years ago. It had been a dark, murky color and I'd stripped it and antiqued it white, working for days until it finally looked like the one in the interior decorator shop window downtown. Would people someday come from all over just to see where Mariah Johnson wrote?

Maybe out of all the guys who came to our beach, there would be one very special one who would smile at me as he was jogging by. Because he would be someone special, I'd smile right back with no trouble at all. Deep inside of me, I've always believed that this trouble about smiling back at boys would completely disappear if the right guy came along.

Yes, the summer would be great! But not perfect. To make it perfect, my father would have to come back—and that was impossible.

I was about twelve when the arguments between my parents started. They would carefully lock the bedroom door at night, but still I could hear their voices rising in anger. Toward the end, my mother would cry a lot. I would finally drift off into a troubled sleep, still hearing my mother's muffled sobs and wondering what it was all about, wishing a miracle would happen and there would be peace between them again.

But it only became worse with time. Finally, on the second day in June, my fourteenth birthday, my father packed his things and walked out. My mother stayed up in her room for a long time after that, and when I went up to try to console her, she wouldn't let me in.

Kim was only four at the time and really didn't realize what was happening. I answered her stupid questions in the rudest, unkindest way. "Shut up and clean up your dirty bedroom," I told her, pushing her in that direction. "Dad will be back. He's got this trip he must take...."

She probably believed me. I even tried to believe the story myself, though for a long time I was really mad at him for picking my birthday, of all times, to leave. He never came back and by the end of the summer the three of us finally settled into a dull routine.

That fall, Mom got a job in a day school where she watched after rich kids. Soon after that she began to talk about going back to college and getting her teaching credentials. Kim went to the school along with Mom and was allowed to attend for half-price because my mother worked there. She stayed there until she entered first grade.

Occasionally envelopes would arrive with my father's return address on them. No letter, just a check to help us over the hard times. That's all I had of my father, a look at his Chicago return address and a trip to the bank to watch my mother cash the check. He rarely wrote or called me, though deep inside I knew he still loved both me and Kim. It was hard for him to come out and say it, though.

Kim wouldn't give up on my father. She drove my mother up the wall, asking her over and over when he would be back. My question was different. I wanted to know why he left in the first place.

One day I got up the courage and asked her point-blank. Kim was busy playing outside that day. My mother had just finished waxing the kitchen floor, her hair tied back in an orange scarf. The question had come as a surprise to her, and if I hadn't caught her off guard, I don't think she would have been so candid.

"He is living in Chicago with a woman he met in his office," she told me, wiping the perspiration from her face. After a while I wondered if any of the tiny beads of sweat were a few stray tears, and I felt sorry that I had pushed the issue. Maybe it would have been better not to know. . . .

I remember saying just one thing to her, "Mom, why don't you ask him to come back—tell him you forgive him?"

"He's happy with her," she said dully. "He doesn't want to come back." I refused to believe that. A man who had my mother for a wife had everything. I'd never believe he actually preferred someone else.

I grabbed my sandals and hopped off my rock when I saw Mom pulling into the driveway. She slammed the old Ford door twice—it never fully closes on the first try—and then waved in my direction. Starting down the hill, she yelled, "Mariah, come help me with the groceries. We've got so much to do!"

I dashed up the hill, and before she had a chance to remove one bag from the car, I was there to help her carry in the bags.

"I have to talk to you and Kim," she said, trying to catch her breath. "They're closing down the school this summer. . . . !"

"But don't they always?" I pointed out, carefully carrying in the bag with the eggs.

"I was counting on them not to," she sighed, opening up the screen door for me. "Back in December they announced they were going to stay open year-round. That way I'd work and get paid during the summer months."

"But we were counting on you just being here, not working." I was aware I sounded like a whining child.

She gave me a funny smile. "It's the money,

Mariah. Of course I'd rather be on a real vacation with you and Kim. I hate to work just as much as anyone, but we need the money to pay the mortgage and all the other bills that pile up. If I'm out of work for a few months, we just won't be able to make it."

"I'll get a job," I told her, my mind racing frantically. "I had a hard time last summer finding anything because I was only fifteen. I'll start searching tomorrow morning."

Just then the kitchen door banged open and Kim came in. The school bus had dropped her right in front of the path under the oleander bushes and from the looks of her, she must have run the length of the path at top speed.

"I'm glad you're here, Kim," my mother called in to her. "I want to talk to you." She led us into the living room.

"I want you to both sit down for a minute," she said, brushing Kim's hair out of her eyes. "I've got some news to tell you.

"It seems we have a problem," she began. "I didn't want to bother you with it, but about three months ago, your father had an auto accident." She quickly added, "Oh, he's really okay now, but he did have a hard time of it. He had to go to the hospital to have some work done on his left leg."

She left the drapes where she had been standing and seated herself in our old oak rocker by the fireplace. "They let him go at the office—he couldn't keep up with the sales force."

Poor Dad, I thought unhappily. I wished I'd known.

She left the rocking chair and walked over to the windows again. My mother loves to look at the waves and whenever she's worried or in deep thought over something, she'll just stare at them for a while. They seem to give her courage to go on, and so Kim and I didn't bother to prod her. We kept very still, just looking at each other.

She walked back to the chair and sat down again, facing us. She looked so terribly tired then. "He hasn't been able to send us any of the support money," she said and her voice was barely a whisper. "I didn't want to scare you, but if we don't get some money from somewhere . . . we might not be able to keep the house."

Kim jumped up and let out a thin shrill noise. I was off of the couch too in a bound, my heart racing madly. "What?" I cried out. I couldn't picture the three of us anyplace else. Not being able to keep the house—to lose it to the bank? No, I couldn't picture it at all!

Mom put up her hand to still our outbursts. "Now, that's what I want to discuss with both of you. There is a way out of this, and I want you to know I've thought it all out carefully. I'm not asking you for your permission. It's beyond that. I'm only asking you to understand my decision." Her words sounded as though she had written them down somewhere and then had spent all day rehearsing them.

"I've accepted a job in Palm Springs. We'll rent out the house here to a very reliable family. Houses along this part of the beach go for very high rent in the summer."

I couldn't believe what she was saying. I couldn't believe this was happening to us—to me! I wouldn't be spending my summer here at all. The novel—what would I do about my novel?

"What position? What job?" My voice sounded like I had a sore throat.

My mother smiled at me, appearing more relaxed. "It's going to be very nice," she went on. "It'll be like an adventure for all of us. Something new. The school has found me a job house-sitting for some people who'll be in Europe all summer."

"House-sitting." Kim laughed and then frowned. "What's house-sitting?"

My mother laughed a little shaky laugh. "Well, to tell you the truth, Kim, I'd never heard of the expression before either, but Mrs. Baker at the school said that it's getting more popular all the time. Very rich people let another person or persons come and live on the property while they're gone. That way they have twenty-four hour security. The house is kept clean and any breakdowns or problems are taken care of. The house where we'll be staying also has a handyman on the premises. Also they mentioned that a young man will be assisting us throughout the summer."

"Who are these rich people?" I asked, still not believing this was happening.

"Abbott," my mother answered. "James and Martha Abbott. Mr. Abbott is a financier. He owns several properties in Palm Springs and two large manufacturing plants in Los Angeles."

Kim started to cry then, and I held my breath so I wouldn't. "But I can't leave here this summer," Kim blurted out. "Judy and I joined the tap-dancing class. We're all signed up!"

I went to the bathroom and pulled some tissues out of the box and took them back to her. Then I had an awful thought. "But who will come and live in our house? Who do we have to rent to?" The thought of anyone sleeping in my bedroom gave me the creeps.

"That's all been arranged, too," my mother said, getting up now and heading for the kitchen. "They're a nice family. When I decided to do this, I posted an ad on the bulletin board at work. In no time at all, one of the mothers contacted me. Her sister has always wanted to come out from Ohio and spend the summer here. She and her husband will be bringing their three children—"

"But, Mom, there must be another way!" I interrupted, watching my mother take some lettuce out of the refrigerator and wash it. "We'll think of something else. There's got to be another way. We can't leave. This summer was going to be important to me!"

My mother carefully placed the lettuce on a folded paper towel, and then she looked at me sternly. "Mariah, you've spent every summer of your life here on this beautiful beach, in this comfortable, lovely home. Now, I'm asking you to give up just one summer. Just one summer so we can stay here the rest of the year. You know very well my solution is the only way." She picked up a can of tuna fish and handed it

21

to me. "Open this," she instructed. "I don't want to talk about it anymore."

Now when my mother says, "I don't want to talk about it anymore," she really means it, so I didn't say anything else. Instead I quickly opened the can, then went into the bathroom and cried.

I reached down, grabbed the tissue and then, standing up again, I caught my reflection in the bathroom mirror. Two definite frown lines seemed permanently etched between my eyes. One tear was already sliding down my right cheek and another was coming down the other cheek, quickly catching up to the first. My mouth hurt from holding it stiff, and even my teeth hurt because I had clamped my jaws together so hard so that I wouldn't say anything more to my mother.

"I'll probably never smile again," I told the sad girl in the mirror.

Chapter 3

"You're not going to take all those books!" I was crouched in the corner of my closet, sorting out my novels when my mother entered my bedroom. I had shot out of bed while it was still dark, hoping I would get a chance to pack all my books, especially the ones by Susan Howatch, and then I'd shove them into the back of the trunk. With a blanket or something spread over them, I'd hoped Mom wouldn't notice them. I knew we needed all the space we could get, but there are some things that should have priority.

"I'm just trying to make more room in the closet," I lied. "For the Gretels and their three kids." I put a heavy accent on the word "three," figuring maybe she would have second thoughts. Three kids could do a lot of damage to a house.

"That's very thoughtful of you, Mariah," my mother said, smiling. "Just stack them up as neatly as you can and come downstairs and help me with the kitchen and living room. My goodness, I didn't realize you had so many books...."

It's a good thing she doesn't know I stacked some in Kim's closet, too, I thought, quickly sliding closed the closet doors. My mother went on with her orders. "The carpet needs a final going over and maybe a quick mop on the kitchen floor, too. They should be here by noon. We'll leave right after they get settled."

The main important thing to me was to get my books into the trunk. Oh, she would find them after we got to Palm Springs, but then it would be too late. As soon as she was out of sight, I grabbed the box I'd hidden the night before and frantically stacked the books as tightly as I could.

Carefully I moved down the staircase, thankful that the thick brown carpeting muffled my steps. Then, as fast as I could, I struggled with the box out to the car.

We keep an old beach towel in the back of the trunk all the time, left over from the trip to Lake Arrowhead we'd taken almost a year ago. I laughed to myself as I carefully tucked the raggedy blue towel around the box, knowing my mother would be too busy to notice.

In a flash I was back in the living room, pushing the vacuum cleaner around like my mother had requested. I finished quickly as my mother flashed by me with a suitcase. "Thanks, Mariah," she said. "Make sure you don't forget any of your clothes. We'll be gone till the week school starts, so pack carefully. But don't overdo it!"

I was halfway up the stairs when I heard my mother's voice. "Mariah!" I knew what was coming. She'd found the books! I ran back down the stairs and headed for the car. She didn't have to say a word, but if looks could kill, I'd be dead right there on the spot.

The box of paperbacks was heavier going up the stairs than coming down. I wondered angrily if Susan Howatch ever had a mother like mine. Here I was, with so much inside of me that wanted to get out, with so much that the publishing world was waiting for—and my own mother was fighting me!

Reluctantly I shoved the box of books in the closet; the old beach towel still on top of them. I sat down on my bed, in the pits of depression. I could hear the waves crashing on the rocks below; sulking, I concentrated on the rhythmic pounding. I was so used to the sound that I never really heard it anymore unless I listened carefully and turned off the rest of the world.

The sound of a car pulling into the driveway jolted me from the bed. They were early! I knew my mother would be upset because she'd wanted more time to get us ready. Looking down from my bedroom window I watched the Gretels climb out of a new, sleek, silver Thunderbird. The car was overflowing with boxes and suitcases—even a bright red surfboard was strapped to its top. I could tell from my upstairs view that the surfboard was brand-new.

If you've ever gone to a circus and watched a whole big bunch of clowns pile out of a little car, you can imagine what the Gretels looked like. The car itself was not terribly small, but they had really overdone it. I couldn't imagine anyone needing all that stuff just to spend a summer at our house.

I watched my mother shake hands with Mr. and Mrs. Gretel. Then I saw two small boys, maybe about six and eight, and a girl with long, blond hair who looked about my age, maybe a year older.

She was about my range in the skinny department, but when she turned I could see her figure was definitely better—there was no doubt about that. And then she stood still and looked up.

Her complexion was like my mother's—a cream color with just the lightest bit of rosiness on her cheeks. A stray lock of yellow hair caught in her mouth when she turned in the ocean breeze, and she quickly pulled it away. Her eyes were a definite blue, like a light blue marble I found on the beach one day, and when she smiled up at me, her white teeth sparkled. She was definitely pretty!

I ducked back out of the window then, knowing I was expected to help out. Kim, ahead of me on the staircase, was terribly excited. "They're here already!"

"I know," I said miserably. Somehow I had hoped they would have changed their minds about the whole thing. Now that they were here, we'd definitely have to leave. It was so final. . . .

Elaine Gretel smiled easily and talked pleasantly to her parents. She seemed all right to me. Her little brothers, on the other hand, pushed and shoved each other all over the place, reminding me of Amy's horrible kid brothers.

"Tony! Mark!" their mother called out every once in a while. "If you don't stop, you'll have to go directly to your room." She was calling one of the bedrooms theirs already!

I helped Elaine upstairs with her suitcases, and we stood in the hall until my mother joined us. "Elaine, you take Mariah's room," she instructed us. "The boys will stay in Kim's."

Well, that was one good thing, I thought, breathing again. I was sure that any girl who looked like Elaine would never ruin any of my things. I had worked so hard for two years now fixing up my bedroom to look just the way it did in one of the magazines. I didn't want some stranger to ruin it all over the summer.

Elaine loved my room right away. She wore worn jeans and a bright red shirt, and she had a white sweater thrown over her shoulders, the sleeves tied around her neck. Her blue beach walkers showed off her soft pink painted toe-nails and when she touched the yellow pillow on my rocking chair, I could see they perfectly matched her neatly manicured fingernails.

I watched her walk over to my vanity with the yellow and white organdy skirt and touch the three mirrors.

"It's great for doing your hair," I told her. "You can see all angles that you might other-wise miss. Sometimes I think I've got it just right but then I'll pull the side mirrors forward a little and see I've got a mess toward the back...."

"I know," Elaine said, but I didn't believe she could ever have trouble with the sides or back of her hair.

27

My mother called me from the downstairs hall. "Come on, Mariah, we don't have all day. I'd like to get on the road before the worst heat hits the desert."

And so my last few moments with my new friend were spent with me running around, making sure I wasn't forgetting anything. I checked the closet and then the drawers, and then quickly scooped up four books. If I didn't have enough time to write one, at least I could study the ones I'd chosen. Quickly I threw them into my straw beach bag where my mother would never find them.

"Goodbye," I said to Elaine. "Have a good summer in my house." And then just as I was about to leave, I had an afterthought. Leading her over to the window, I pointed out a group of black rocks where the sea gulls were sitting.

"That's a good place to sit and think and to really be alone. I sit there quite a lot."

Elaine smiled and touched me lightly on the shoulder. "I guess I'm a lot like you. Sometimes I need to be alone, too. Thanks for showing me your rock."

I never thought I'd see the day that I'd share my rock with anyone.

Chapter 4

It took us about one and a half hours to get to Palm Springs, and that's just about how long I sulked. Kim sat in the back of the car, surrounded by boxes, her nose in her coloring book.

Finally we got off the freeway and turned onto a narrow road. It wasn't terribly narrow, of course, but it seemed so after the freeway. On the left of us, we could see flat desert land; on the right of us, mountains with a haze around them, making them look almost purple.

"Early in the year you can see snow up on top of those mountains," my mother told us. "Those tiny sticks up there that look like toothpicks—they're really huge evergreens."

"Can we go up on the tram?" Kim asked, noting a huge sign on the side of the road, advertising the cable cars that go to the top of the mountain.

"We'll see," she said.

We passed the sign that says, The Palm Springs Aerial Tramway, and then we entered the town of Palm Springs. Another sign, Visit The Indian Canyons—Chamber of Commerce, Palm Springs. I didn't even know there were Indians in Palm Springs.

29

Mom pulled the car into a Sambo parking lot. "Let's eat now and then consult the map Mr. Abbott sent me."

"You mean we have to go further than this?" asked the impatient Kim.

"Not much further," my mother said, "but I'm hungry, and we should freshen up before we reach the house."

"But there's no one there—much," I said. "The Abbotts have already left for Europe."

The place was so crowded we had to wait for a booth. "I didn't know so many people came to Palm Springs in the summer," I said, watching the busy waitresses rushing around.

"I hear it is getting to be quite popular," my mother told me. "With everything air-conditioned, people don't mind the heat. Most of the time they sit around their gorgeous pools anyway. A lot of people come here just to rest, you know."

Bor-ing, I thought, but I didn't say it out loud. If we had to go through with it, and standing in Sambo's gave me the feeling that we were there already, I might as well stop sulking and try to be pleasant. But I missed our house already....

The waitress was serving another cup of coffee to my mother when my mother pulled out a crude map drawn by hand.

"We'd better go now," she said after examining the map. "The handymen are probably wondering where we are. Let's see," she went on, "Mr. Abbott wrote it down for me someplace...

30

oh, yes, one is called Old Jim—just that—no last name. He's almost seventy. And the other one is Paul. Paul Strobe. 'Just turned eighteen—and a delightful boy,' Mr. Abbott wrote. Well, I'm sure both of them will be helpful."

I finished the last of my Coke. Eighteen. My straw made a bubbly sound as I breathed up the last of the drink. An eighteen-year-old guy from town, making summer money at Mr. Abbott's mansion. Maybe I'd practice my smile on him. . . .

Neat little stores lined both sides of Palm Canyon Drive. Bookstores, lots of clothing shops, florists, interior decorating shops, just about everything you could possibly think of. I was glad there were bookstores. I'd find a way to get away from the Abbotts' house and check them out.

The shopping district was several blocks long and a few minutes later I spotted the library. I smiled. They'd get to know me there this summer as a tourist who loved to rummage around their dusty books. Later, maybe later I'd find enough time to drop in—as a well-known writer. Just the thought sent a chill up and down my spine.

Eventually we came to a sign posted on a fence post. "Skipalot Drive—Private Road," Kim read. "I like that name." She said it several times over and over and over. I felt like bopping her.

I could feel the hot air and sand mixing in

my throat, as a sudden wind had come up and swirled around our car, causing the sand to fly in the windows.

"There it is ahead," my mother called out to us. I was amazed she could see anything at all. She slowed the car down.

The first house loomed up in the windshield and I could see a wooden sign swinging from a wrought iron post. Abbott, it said. Actually you couldn't see too much of the house from the road because of the massive stone wall surrounding it. There was a wall surrounding the other house down the road, the only other one in sight. But you could tell they were both magnificent mansions.

Tall, majestic date palms swayed on all sides of the walls, like sentries guarding the hidden castles. The road went all the way up to the second mansion and then came to a dead end.

My mother stopped the car in front of the Abbott sign and just sat and stared at the iron gate. Finally she crawled out of the car.

She tugged at a black box that turned out to be a phone and then she found a buzzer. After pressing it for a moment, a voice came from out of the box. It was a young voice, a boy's—not Old Jim, for sure, I thought.

"Yes-s?"

"We're here," my mother said into the little black box. "The Johnsons." She blushed a little and smiled at us.

"Wow!" Kim said, peering out of the car window. "They must have scads of money!"

"Hush," my mother said, putting her finger

up to her lips. "They can probably hear every-thing we say."

All of a sudden the gates began to slowly slide open. Quickly my mother ran back to the car and started the motor.

"No telling just how long that thing will stay open," she said, driving the car into the opening.

Inside the gates, we approached a semi-circular driveway with masses of flowers and different kinds of cactus and date palms sur-rounding it. They would have to have a full-time gardener, I thought, gasping at the beauty of the place.

The house was a Spanish villa—like some-thing I'd seen in a magazine once. The outside was a light salmon color, covered by lush green vines. A tilted veranda surrounded the first floor, and when I walked on the tiles, I felt like I was walking over someone's hand-painted pic-tures. Each tile was so different, but the minia-ture flowers in each were blue and white with green leaves.

The second floor was surrounded by its own porches. From the ledges I could see huge clay pots filled with pink and white and purple geraniums.

The mammoth, heavily carved wooden front door swung open and a boy stretched out his hand in greeting.

Paul Strobe.

He was wearing a faded blue T-shirt and jeans, but that's not what I saw first, I must admit. His hair hung over one eye and he pushed it back like it was a habit. I would write in my notebook later that his hair was the color of the sand I had seen for miles—blond with light brown streaks. It looked so soft, I wanted to reach out and touch it. His eyes were the deep blue of a summer sky, and his smile was so natural and sincere, it was infectious.

I sucked in my breath and extended my hand when it came my turn. I felt the warmth of his hand, a warmth that stayed even after he turned to shake Kim's hand. The touch had created a tiny tingle of electricity that reached the insides of my heart. . . .

Chapter 5

"You're lucky there's a buzzer hook-up out back," Paul said, smiling again at my mother. "With all the noise Jim and I are making out back, we would have never heard you."

His nose was very straight and just the right length. His skin was evenly tanned and the longer I looked at his eyes, the bluer they seemed to become. I felt the red rushing to my face—surely he could feel me staring at him. Looking down at the tiles, I pretended to study them. I didn't raise my head up until he was finally ushering us inside.

We walked on glistening white marble slabs inside the vestibule. At the end of the hallway there was a magnificent staircase all in white. We'd have to go around without shoes, I thought.

Turning then to the left, Paul led us into a sunken living room, its thick, deep blue carpeting swallowing up our feet. I swear I couldn't see below my ankles when I looked down.

"I'll have to give you a quickie tour," Paul said, wiping a streak of ivory paint from his arm. It got on his hand and when he pushed back his hair again, he'd transferred some to his forehead. I laughed out loud, causing him to take a look in the gilt-edged mirror over the stone fireplace. I breathed a sigh of relief when he laughed, too.

"What a creepy sight I am," he told us. "But like I said, it'll have to be a real quick tour as I don't want Jim out in that hot sun alone too long or he'll just keep right on working until he drops over."

"Are you gardening?" my mother asked, still stunned by the plush room.

"We're building a gazebo," Paul told us, taking a rag out of his back pocket. He tried to wipe the paint from his forehead, but only smudged it further.

"What's a gazebo?" Kim asked.

"I'll show you when we go outside," Paul answered her, and he reached out and tousled her hair. He stood tall; I tried to figure out the inches between my height and his and I would guess he stood about six feet. He was skinny, too, but I knew he had some good-looking muscles under that shirt. A shudder went through me as I thought about that.

It seemed so funny that someone was showing us a house. Just a few hours ago we were showing our house to the Gretels. Our little tour had taken just a few minutes, but this one would take a lot more. Maybe we'd never get to see it all!

The Abbott house had six bedrooms upstairs and three down and each one had its own bathroom and sitting room. The kitchen was as big as our entire downstairs at home and had its own fireplace. The dining room was as formal as the living room, and I knew we would never, never eat there unless we planned to entertain royalty.

Then Paul led us to Mr. Abbott's study. It was somewhat like a library, with leather everywhere—even on the walls! Another room Paul called the "unwinding room." In there was a pool table made out of white marble, a television with a screen so large, I thought we were in a private theater, a shelf full of all kinds of computer games, and a huge stereo sound system that covered an entire wall. Wherever you looked there were paintings of boats and fishermen.

Fresh flowers were everywhere—in ornate Chinese vases on massive slabs of wood Paul called coffee tables and in magnificent containers in various shapes on all the fireplace mantels. (There were six fireplaces throughout the house.)

"You'll like Old Jim—Jim Cable," Paul told us, winding up the inside tour. "Mr. Abbott calls him his 'lifesaver.' He's a man of many talents—gardener, carpenter. They rarely have to call a plumber unless the job gets too complicated. Jim also fixes little things, like a broken rocking chair or a lamp."

We stepped outside onto a patio made of brick-on-sand. There were flowers everywhere (now I knew where they got all of those flowers for all of those vases). Palm trees of all sizes graced the back garden, and following the red, brick path, we suddenly came upon an enormous oval-shaped swimming pool. It looked like a dark, rock-rimmed lagoon, with a gently trickling waterfall and literally hundreds of plants around it.

"It's like a jungle," I gasped. "And the pool looks like something you'd stumble upon in paradise...."

"The tiles in the pool are a smoky black," Paul told us. "And the bottom and the sides are painted black."

My mother peered down into the water. "The illusion really makes you forget that this lush garden is really in the heart of the desert," she said, turning back to Paul. "And what are all those?" she asked pointing at the jungle itself.

"Agaves, aloes, bananas, oleanders, palms," Paul said. "And over here, palms, sedums, and yuccas. It took a long, long time to make it look like this."

Paul led us past the pool and further into the jungle of flowers until we came to a clearing stacked with wood and cans of paint.

An old man was sawing a piece of wood with some kind of electric saw. He switched it off as soon as he heard us coming. "Hello-o," he called out to us, smiling. "I'm Jim," he said, extending a blue-veined, wrinkled hand.

My mother took it warmly and smiled back. He shook our hands so hard, it was like he was pumping for water. He smiled wider, and I could see more spaces than teeth.

"Jim lives in the little house beyond those trees," Paul explained. "Trudy, the maid, is off for the entire summer and also Rachel, the cook, will be gone until September. Jim has decided to spend the summer here, though."

"I don't have no place better to go," Jim said laughing. His face was wrinkled like a dried-up apple, and there were about six gray-brown hairs on his crinkly head.

"We are lucky then," my mother said to him. He smiled a broad smile that made his wrinkles break out into more wrinkles. I liked him right from the very start.

"What we're doing here," Paul went on, pointing to the clearing, "is a secret, a surprise for Mrs. Abbott. She's wanted a gazebo all of her life and Mr. Abbott asked us to build it while they were off on their trip. We couldn't start on it until last week after they left."

"We told her we were clearin' this place for a hothouse," Jim told us. "When she sees the gazebo, she'll darn right keel over!"

"I was just experimenting with the paint," Paul said, applying turpentine to a rag and then rubbing off the smudge. Then he leaned over and washed his skin with clear water. "That should do it," he said, forgetting about the paint on his forehead.

"Okay," my mother said to Kim and me. "Let's go inside and start putting our things away."

I looked back one more time as I left the clearing, at all of the stacked wood and paint they were to use on the project. It looked like a big job which meant I would be seeing a lot of Paul Strobe. Things were looking up, I thought, as I reentered the Abbott house. Maybe Palm Springs wouldn't be so bad after all.

Chapter 6

I begged my mother to allow me to stay in an upstairs bedroom.

"That's foolish," she told me, unpacking her clothes in one of the downstairs bedrooms. "You'll spend all your time climbing up and down those endless stairs! The bedrooms on the first floor are so beautiful!"

"I want the one with the peacocks on the walls," Kim said. "There's a nice window where I can see clear out to the pool."

"The Abbotts said we could use any of the rooms except for their bedroom in the east wing," my mother reminded us. "I suppose you could take one of those other rooms up there, Mariah, but why, when there's that lovely green and white one next to mine?"

She had no way of knowing that I had already inspected each bedroom thoroughly. There was one with a backyard view and a window seat that I just couldn't resist. Propped up against the rose-colored velvet pillows on the wide windowsill I could watch progress on the gazebo (and see some more of this Paul Strobe, too).

About one hour later, after I'd unpacked all my clothes, showered, and changed into a fresh green shirt and white shorts, I checked my mother's room and then Kim's. Both of them had fallen asleep in the middle of their beds. I made my way to the back door. I knew Paul was still out there, with the blueprints spread in front of him, placing different sizes of wood into different stacks; Old Jim had finally left, to take an afternoon nap, I guessed. I had seen it all from my perch in the window seat.

I touched the back door to open it, and then swung around, looking for a pitcher. I'd have to bring him some water—or something, I figured. Peeking into the refrigerator, I whistled when I saw how really big it was inside. I'd never seen anything like it—even in the stores. "Wow," I said under my breath. "It's big enough for a restaurant!"

There were several cartons of Coke, root beer, diet drinks, and orange juice in bottles. I grabbed two ice-cold Cokes and closed the door.

I took one last peek at myself in a mirror over the sink, and with my fingernails I tried to dig out a few strands of hair, trying to make them whispy looking so that I wouldn't look *too* neat. What I wanted to get was a kind of tousled I-don't-care-look, so he wouldn't know how long and carefully I had brushed my hair.

"Oh, well," I said in despair to the mirror. "If you don't have anything to work with—what can you expect!"

It looked like I had caught Paul just as he was leaving, and my hopes slid into the pits. "Oh, you're done for the day?" I asked stupidly as he was removing his work gloves.

He looked up and smiled so that all of his beautiful teeth showed. There was nothing wrong with *his* smile, I thought. Oh, how lucky to respond so easily to people. My hand shook as I held out a friendly cold Coke to him.

"Whew," he said, wiping his brow with the back of his hand. "You're an angel—how did you know I was parched? I didn't think I'd make it home."

He tilted his head back and took one long drink. I could see his Adam's apple sliding up and down. "Come on, Mariah," he said. No one had ever, ever said my name so smoothly. "Let's sit around the pool. It's cooler there." His blue eyes peered intently into mine as he spoke. I'd have done anything he said at that point.

We took our drinks to the edge of the deep part and he threw himself down on the cool bricks. I couldn't help but admire his long, slender fingers. An artist's hand, I thought, my imagination running wild. For a few moments there was silence. I panicked—I'd have to say something quick or he'd think I was a real jerk! "I just think it's great, you and Old Jim building a gazebo," I said, my voice shaking, but then gaining in strength.

"I love gazebos," I went on. "I've always loved them. They're found in so many gardens in England. I mean, they're so Victorian. . . ."

"That's true," he said. "Actually though they go back as far as early Egypt."

"There are so many designs to choose from," I added, glad that I had done my homework in the Abbotts' study. I wouldn't mind if he thought

I wasn't pretty, because I couldn't do anything at all about that, but at least I could be well informed.

"True," he said again, rising up on one elbow to look at me directly. "Old Jim and I went through loads of books before we came across this one. Mr. Abbott agreed this was the best. Then we had to send away for the plans and order the materials. It took us an entire week just to clear the area of plants."

He took another long drink. "It always amazes me to see what you can do with a pile of wood and some nails and a little paint."

"Then you want to be a carpenter?"

"No, an architect," he answered, finishing his Coke. His shirt stuck to his back from the heat. "That's my dream," he went on. "And it's coming closer with each day. September I start at Berkeley. Later on I hope to finish up at MIT."

"Wow," I said, sounding like my little sister. I finished my Coke, too. "You really mean it? I mean that place is expensive." What a dumb thing to say, I thought after the words left my mouth.

"I know," he said, pretending my question wasn't dumb. "But it's a career, a profession, a lifetime. In the field of architecture you have to get every bit of education you can. That's if you want to be a good one."

He stared into the pool, his wrist dangling the empty Coke can in a swirling motion. I got the feeling that this Paul Strobe was as serious about his career as I was about my writing. We sat there, on the edge of the water, not talking,

43

just sitting there in the sun together. I felt strangely at ease, relaxed, as though I was sitting with someone I'd known all of my life. Was it the same for him?

He looked down at his watch after a few minutes. "I've got to get home," he said. "My mom is the type who says you're late if you're only thirty seconds later than you said you'd be. She's a worrier."

"All mothers worry," I told him, laughing. And then as an afterthought, "What are the Abbotts like? I mean they're so terribly rich—are they nice people? I mean, do you like them yourself?"

"They're fantastic," Paul answered, turning to me, his blue eyes looking straight into mine. I felt my throat grow dry, even after the coldness of the Coke. "I've known them all of my life and when they found out I was interested in carpentry, Mr. Abbott introduced me to Jim. That was years ago when I could barely hold a hammer. Jim actually started me with an old play hammer and some wood scraps he had in the back shed.

"He taught me everything he knew. Then, when Mr. Abbott found out that I wanted to be an architect, he encouraged me, even more than my own dad. Mrs. Abbott is great, too. It's amazing I'm not fat, with all the cooking and baking she does. Here she has all these servants, and she still loves her kitchen. Yeah—they're fantastic!"

A tiny breeze came up, pushing a strand of hair into my face and I brushed it away. "I'm surprised. I mean—rich people—they're not usually too nice," I told him. "My mother teaches in a very ritzy day school and there are some really rich kids there. My mom says they're spoiled brats, and when their folks come in for interviews, it's disgusting how uppity they are. And me, I know some rich kids from school. I wouldn't give a dime for them. I mean they're just so.... I guess the word is 'shallow.' "

Paul stared back into the pool as he put his feet over the side and dunked them. He was silent for a moment. "Maybe if you got to know them better," he said finally. "Maybe it's kind of your fault, too. I mean, you look at them already knowing you're not going to like them. Do you suppose it could be that?"

I laughed nervously. "Oh, Paul, you're wrong. You just happen to know a few rich people who *are* nice, but if you knew the ones I've met!" I shook my head knowingly.

The water looked cool and tempting, and I removed my sandals and dipped my toes in, too. "Okay, besides the Abbotts, just who else do you know? I mean someone who is really, really rich and is just as nice as they are?" I challenged him.

Paul bent back and looked up at the blue sky. A fluffy white cloud drifted directly above his head. He seemed to be thinking very hard.

After a second I said, "Ha! You see, you can't even think of one!"

"No, you're wrong," he said, removing his feet from the water. "Did you notice the other house on this street?"

"How could I avoid seeing it?" I said. "It's huge, and I bet as fancy as this one. Why?"

"I know the people who live there, too," Paul said. "Especially the guy my age. He's pretty nice, I'd say. Yes, I can say I really like him. Maybe you'd like to meet him."

I shook my head. "No, thank you. I wouldn't want to. Besides I wouldn't know exactly how to talk to him. Rich people seem to always put on airs. You know, they make me feel terribly small, inferior."

He stood up then, and I got to my feet too. "Well, like I said, I've got to get home for dinner."

He walked a few feet over to a clump of oleander and pulled out a red and white moped. "I'll be here tomorrow again, Mariah. If you have any free time, maybe you could help me and Old Jim. . . . I mean if you'd care too." He smiled, again, that heavenly wonderful smile.

I could feel myself smile, and I wondered if I looked like a nerd. I quickly made my face straight again. "Yes, I really would like that," I told him, trying to hide the emotion I felt in my heart.

He waved at me and left the garden area by a gate in the stone wall that I hadn't seen before. I could hear the moped begin its putting noise and then heard it fade away in the distance. I looked up to see the sun easing itself over to the west. It would be a long time until it finally set, and I had met a boy already. Someone I could talk to, be really comfortable with. I hoped, oh, how I hoped I hadn't looked stupid

46

or said anything to turn him off. I headed for the house and vowed I'd try to set my hair with a little more care that night. I thought of Amy. Amy would just die if I told her about Paul!

Chapter 7

"Oh, darn!" I said.

"What's wrong now?" my mother asked as she entered my bedroom the next morning.

"I don't have Amy's address!" I moaned.

"She's visiting her father in New York, isn't she? Why don't you just pick up the phone and call her mother?" my mother asked.

"Can't," I said, flinging my letter paper onto the bedspread. "She's gone, too. She took Amy's brothers back to Iowa for the whole summer. Boy, I wanted so badly to write to Amy, too... especially now."

"Why especially now?" my mother asked, her very, very sharp mind absorbing my last statement.

I floundered for words. "I want to tell her about this great house and all."

My mother smiled smugly. "Yes," she said, going over to the window seat. "Yes, this great house and *all*." She picked up a pillow and fluffed it up. "Mariah, why don't we invite the *and all* to a barbeque tonight?"

"Who's having a barbeque?" Kim yelled up from downstairs. The kid should get an award for her fantastic hearing, I thought. In seconds she was at my bedroom door. "What barbe-que?"

My mother laughed and fluffed up the pillows on the window seat. "Ask Mariah," she said, her smile turning into a mischievous grin.

Sliding my stationery back into the drawer in the walnut desk, I turned to my little sister. "She means Old Jim," I told her, evading my mother's surprised look. "We could have dinner tonight after the sun goes down—right out back on that neat brick patio."

"Great!" Kim said. "And we could invite Paul Strobe, too!"

My mother and I took one look at each other and without another word we were laughing, laughing so hard, I could feel tears popping out of the corners of my eyes. She came over to the desk and put a hand on my shoulder.

"Why not, Mariah? Why don't you ask Paul?" She was serious.

"I'll ask him," Kim volunteered, and I heaved a sigh of relief.

My mother smiled. "You're off the hook," she said in a whisper so Kim couldn't hear. And then she turned to my little sister. "You do that, Kim, right this morning so he can let his folks know."

Kim was out of the bedroom in a streak, and my mother returned to the window seat. I watched her arrange herself among the rose-colored pillows. She was enjoying my bird's-eye view as I had done the day before. She looked so beautiful in the morning sunlight, and so terribly young, almost like me, I thought. Had she been shy with boys herself when she was my age? I doubted it. She had been pretty, very pretty then, not like me with my plain face and brown-green eyes that kept on changing colors.

I was still having trouble in the makeup department. I couldn't keep lipstick on very long—I was always biting it off. And my hair—my hair was the worst of all. Maybe I'd be able to do something with it someday, but right now it seemed no matter what I did, it still wanted to hang straight. Maybe I could talk Mom into giving me a perm. It couldn't hurt.

My mother interrupted my thoughts. "Let's get the housework done quickly so we can enjoy the rest of the day," she said. "I want you and Kim to go to the supermarket with me. Maybe we'll have time to visit some of those cute shops, too."

As soon as she left the room I dashed over to the window seat and caught Kim just as she was approaching Paul. I couldn't hear their voices, of course, but I pretty well could tell what they were saying. Kim spoke first, and then I could see a smile cross Paul's face as he nodded his head. He was coming! Old Jim was being asked next and he smiled in turn. He looked perfectly delighted.

I felt the blood rushing to my face and I put my hands over the warmness even though no one was around. No matter what happened that day, it would never be as wonderful as the evening to come promised to be. Quickly I took one more look at the skinny, gangly girl in the mirror—and then I was off to tour the big downtown of little Palm Springs.

"I wanted to do the food shopping first," my mother said, as she drove to the downtown area, "but the food'll spoil in the heat, so, let's give the stores a quick going-over first."

The shops along the main street were immaculate. I learned later that all of the shopkeepers hose down the sidewalks in front of their stores every morning. Each little shop sparkles with spotless windows, and their displays are breathtaking. Some of them were closed for the season, but most of them welcomed their customers with open doors and soft music playing inside. We passed the library again and I made a mental note to visit there as soon as I could break away.

It was almost three-thirty when we finally got back to the Abbotts'. After I helped my mother put away the groceries, I ran upstairs, freshened my face, brushed my hair, and then dashed out to the backyard. If I had just taken the time to look out from the window seat, I would have seen the beginnings of a gazebo— with no one in sight.

Too late, I thought, as I entered the empty clearing. "Howdy," Jim saluted me, coming from behind the oleanders. "If you've come to help out, that's fine, Mariah."

"But there's no one here," I blurted out.

"Well, there's me." He chuckled. "No, I get what you mean. Paul just left for a few seconds. He had to run back to his house to pick up some boxes of nails."

"Oh," I said, sitting down on a pile of wood. "Just where does he—how far away is his house? When we left the main road and started up Skipalot Drive, I didn't see a sign of any other houses, except these two big ones."

Jim gave me a funny look. "Thought you knowed," he said, slipping on his work gloves. He bent over and picked up a piece of wood that would go into the gazebo's decking. "Paul lives in that other big house. Yeh, I thought you knowed."

My mouth hung open and my mind twirled in confusion. No, I hadn't "knowed." Paul must really hate me—or at least think I'm a real jerk. Why didn't he tell me? Before I could say a word to Jim, Paul entered the clearing with several boxes of nails in his hands.

"Hi," he called out to me. "Good, you can help pound some nails. Jim, where's the other hammer?"

"I can't stay," I said, and my voice sounded like it belonged to someone else. "I have to help my mother." And with that, I turned and ran out of the clearing, past the jungle of flowers, past the pool, and then finally through the kitchen door. I was going so fast I slammed headlong into my mother, who caught me by the arm and swung me around.

"Hey, honey, what's the hurry? You look so white. Are you sick?"

"Yes," I told her. "I'm sick and humiliated and angry and embarrassed and disappointed."

"Whew," she said, settling the broom against

the kitchen cupboards. "Would you like to tell me what's wrong?"

I threw myself down on a kitchen chair and watched as my mother turned up the flame under the coffeepot. She and I always sat down in the kitchen at home and drank coffee together whenever we had something bothering us. Somehow our little talks together always seemed to help, and the good strong coffee she made warmed my insides and melted away the problem.

"He led me to believe he was a—worker—you know, like one of us."

"What on earth are you talking about?" she asked, sliding into a chair. "You're not making any sense."

"Yesterday we talked about people with money, rich people. Paul could have told me then that he was one of them, but did he? No. He just led me on and I said"—my face grew hot when I remembered exactly what I had said—"I told him that I had never met a really rich person that I could like. Then I went on about the rich kids and parents you have to put up with."

"And what did he say?"

"He just said that maybe I was wrong. Maybe I didn't take the time or effort to know them. But he could have said right then and there that he was rich himself."

"Well, just how rich is he? I mean, how did you find out?"

"Jim told me. Paul Strobe lives in the mansion next door."

My mother's eyes opened wider and she said, "Whew," breathing out a little whistle. "Yes, that's rich, no doubt about it," she added.

"The thing is, Mom, he let me go on and on, making a fool of myself—so that he could laugh at me later when I did find out!" I shook my head in anger.

"Well, then, you've learned a lesson," she said, getting up to pour our coffee. I could see I'd get no sympathy from her. I stared in disbelief. "Maybe we shouldn't be so quick to label people by the money they have or don't have."

My mind was confused. I sipped around the edges of the coffee cup and my face felt cooler. "You don't think he was making fun of me, deceiving me?" I said.

My mother laughed. "No, dear. I like him too much to think that of him. Tonight you ought to apologize to him for the things you said."

"I'm not going," I whined.

"Mariah, you're always saying you want to write. There are a lot of words you must learn for your vocabulary and one is—apologize. Don't just learn how to spell it. Use it. Feel it, try it on for size and I guarantee you'll be a better writer."

"Okay, I'll go," I said glumly.

She had convinced me, but it was still going to be uncomfortable; I just hoped she wasn't wrong. I looked at the clock. In just a matter of four hours I'd face Paul again—if he came again, I thought. Maybe he just wouldn't show up. Well, anyway, in four more hours I'd know.

Chapter 8

I started the fire and told Kim to set the picnic table out on the patio.

"Make sure there are dishes of pickle relish, mustard, catsup, and anything else you can think of," I told her. "I don't want us to have to run in and out for anything." Kim nodded and set to work.

But my mind was far from the pickle relish or hot dogs at that moment. *Maybe he wouldn't show up.* It was ten after eight already and neither Jim nor Paul had arrived. I stared into the fire as it flared in sharp wild points of white, leaping for the dark sky, and then slowly quieted down and burned slow and steady. Soon the coals would turn gray and it would be time for the hot dogs. Still Paul did not show.

My mother came out with the hot dogs and rolls and at the same time, Jim was coming down the brick path. He had a paper bag in his hand, and he thrust it at my mother. "They're still hot," he said. "Right from the oven."

My mother opened the bag and smiled. "Chocolate chip cookies," she exclaimed. "We love them! Where did you . . . did you make these yourself?"

"Sure did," Old Jim said, smiling and showing where some teeth should be. "Right after I gave up the gazebo today."

"I didn't know you could bake, too," my mother told him.

"My wife and me used to bake all the time," he told us. His voice sounded so wistful, trailing off in not more than a whisper. I knew my mother wouldn't probe further because the timing wasn't right. When he wanted to, he would tell us. My mother was very smart that way. She knew just when to question people and when to leave them alone. Not like me, I realized.

At eight-thirty I sneaked a glance at my mother. She didn't say anything, but I knew she was thinking the same thing I was—*he wasn't going to show.*

"I think we should start the hot dogs," my mother said at eight forty-five. "You must be starved," she said to Jim.

"That I am," the old man said, drinking his second cup of coffee. He'd brought a bottle of something with him and every once in a while he would slip it out of his back pocket and add it to his coffee. My mother pretended she didn't notice, but I knew she did.

As the sound of the hot dogs sizzling on the grill filled the air, I looked up and gazed glumly at the stars. Palm Springs weather is really strange. No matter how hot it is in the day, it gets beautiful and cool at night. I would call all the nights heavenly, because you can see every star you'll ever want to see. And there are a lot of strange noises, including coyotes, Jim had told us. And then the birds. Did they never sleep? In the Abbotts' garden they talked among themselves all night.

Suddenly the bushes swayed and parted and Paul Strobe stood before us. Trying to catch his breath, he said to all of us, "I'm sorry I'm late. I wanted to buy a few things, and the store was jammed."

He handed my mother a box of chocolates and a huge bag of M & M's to Kim. In his other hand he carried a bag and he handed that one to me. "It's a book," he said, trying to catch his breath. "I picked it up in Dad's bookstore. It's all about Palm Springs and I think you'll really enjoy it."

Slowly I pulled it out of the bag. I opened it carefully and saw it contained the complete history of the city, and a list of things for the present and then a chapter on the future of the town. There were at least twenty pages of paintings of the desert and the Indians. It was beautiful. But more importantly, if he gave me a book, that must mean he doesn't hate me! My heart felt as if a ton of bricks had been lifted off of it.

"It tells all about the Indians, their reservations, how Palm Springs was formed. You'll enjoy it, I'm sure," Paul told me.

"Thank you," I said, cheerfully. "I'll look at it before I go to bed."

"Paul should show you the canyons," Old Jim said, sipping at his coffee. "Oh, but I forgot, it's summer and they're closed to the public."

Paul stood before me; he hadn't moved an

inch since he had presented his gift to me. "I'll show her anyway," he said to Old Jim. And then to me, "I have a secret entrance; my friend Joe showed me. But then, I'll tell you about it later."

Later. I savored the sweet sound of that word. He wanted to take me to the canyons, to talk to me—later. I looked up into his face, his blue eyes twinkling with friendliness. I blushed when he answered my starry-eyed stare with a quick wink.

"They're on fire!" My mother was yelling, pointing at the hot dogs revolving on the spit. "Let's get them off!" She ran over to remove them and Jim followed to help. Kim had disappeared into the oleanders, and I knew she was stealing some of the M & M's before dinner, ignoring my mother's warning that she not open the bag until she'd eaten.

Paul and I sat down at the far end of the picnic bench, far enough away from the others so they wouldn't hear. I took a deep breath and looked straight ahead.

"I'm sorry," I whispered to him. "I'm sorry I bad-mouthed rich people in front of you. I had no way of knowing."

He put up his hand. "No, I should have come right out with it. I should be apologizing. That's why I brought the book to you—it's a peace offering."

"But if I had known—"

"It's okay, Mariah. Remember what I said about that guy who lives in that house? He's so nice he wants to show you that all rich people aren't snobs." He tweaked my nose playfully.

I laughed, hoping the others wouldn't notice. "Still, I was wrong," I repeated.

"Look, Mariah, I'm not rich," he said seriously. "My great-grandfather came to Palm Springs and knocked himself out on the land to make a good living. Later on he bought parcels of the land and became rich. Then his son, my grandfather, worked right along with him. Then my father inherited it all and bought a book shop and sold properties—and there you are. I'm just my father's son. So far I haven't made a dime of that wealth, but I'm going to work hard and be something my folks will be proud of."

Here I had worried all that time about apologizing to Paul and it hadn't been hard at all. I smiled at him. Under the picnic table, he found and squeezed my hand.

My mother and Jim came over to the table with the charred hot dogs just as Kim conveniently stepped out of the oleanders. But before they all reached the table, Paul whispered to me, "You have a beautiful smile, Mariah. A beautiful smile...."

Chapter 9

I lay awake for hours that night touching my mouth, my face, getting up several times and looking in the hand mirror on the chest of drawers. It was like a miracle. In one short day, I had turned pretty. It wasn't just my imagination either, because the mirror proved it. Just the night before I'd been practicing my smile, and it had been just as rigid as it had always been. But Paul had said my smile was beautiful—and sure enough, now it was.

As I tossed and turned, I thought of Paul, and I wondered if he thought about me at all. Then just before I drifted off to sleep, I thought of Elaine, the girl in my bed, in my own house.

Was she sleeping or did she toss and turn like me, listening to the night noises in a strange place? Would the sound of the waves crashing on the rocks below keep her awake? Would the two cats next door whine all night and bother her? Had she met someone, too?

"Maybe I'll write to her." I sat up in bed and said out loud. "Why not?" I yawned and fell back on the pillows. First thing, after breakfast, I'd dash off a few lines. I fell asleep at last.

It was the very next day that I found the letter from my father. It happened early in the morning, right after breakfast. My mother had intended to help us weed a geranium patch near the pool. "Would you run in and get my orange scarf?" she asked me. "The sun makes my hair dry."

I should wear one, too, I thought. That was one of her secrets for beautiful hair. I ran to her bedroom, wishing I could drag the air conditioner outside with me.

The scarf was in the top drawer of the chest, right near the bed, but when I entered the room my eyes strayed over to the bed. There on the velvet patchwork bedspread, I saw the pieces of paper, and instantly recognized the handwriting. My father's.

I knew the letter wasn't for me, but I couldn't stop reading. I'll just scan it, the better part of my soul said. But the other part won, and I sank down on the bed and read it from beginning to end.

He wanted to return to us, he said. He wanted to be a good father and husband. He said he had been a terrible fool to leave us and he begged my mother to let him come back. He pleaded so hard, I felt the tears spring to my eyes. "I've asked so many, many times," he wrote. "Why can't you forgive me?"

My eyes darted up to the date on the letter— January 8. The letter was an old one! Way back in January he was asking to come back! And all of this time my mother was telling me that he didn't want to! Why?

My eyes stung with hot tears as I placed the letter back on the bed exactly as I had found it. I wouldn't mention it, of course, but my heart ached so painfully, I hoped it would never show in my face.

Pulling the orange scarf out of the drawer, I headed back to my mother, my heart feeling like one of the patio bricks.

The next few days were so busy, it was well into the next week before I finally got a chance to write to Elaine. Almost all of the daylight hours were spent either on the gazebo or weeding the flower beds. Since Jim could not devote his time to the garden, Kim and I had to. The weeds were hideous, and the sun too bright. Kim and I worked in our bathing suits so that whenever we got too hot, we'd take a quick plunge in the pool. We also had to wear T-shirts to protect our backs from getting broiled.

At lunchtime my mother would call us and we'd eat on the picnic bench. Most of the time Paul joined us, although he devoted at least three hours of each day to helping his parents in the book shop. We never got to spend any time alone, however, and I wondered if he'd ever show me Palm Springs as he promised. I also wondered what he did at night.

The gazebo was coming along nicely. Jim had stacked up his hand-carved railings against another pile of wood, and his latticework was almost completed.

Finally I was able to help when it came to the painting. Jim, Paul, and I carefully applied the ivory paint on the structure, Jim standing back once in a while and saying, "It's good. We made ourselves a pretty good gazebo!"

Paul stood back, brush in hand, his face sweating in the heat. His smile was broad and his blue eyes sparkled with the satisfaction of a job well done. "I love it," he shouted. "Yeah, we did all right!"

They had good reason for being proud. The little clearing, boxes of nails, bricks for the foundation under the wooden platform, and the paint had produced a most beautiful round sun porch. The hand-carved railings and cornice and latticework were interwoven like lace, and the cedar shingles covered a carousel-type roof. When I stood back and surveyed it all, a lump suddenly stuck in my throat.

I could almost see a lady with a parasol, way back in the Victorian days, running through the flowers, tiptoeing up the two steps to the platform. She swung around, seated herself on the cushions on the bench seats, and in seconds, a man followed her up the steps. Together they sat there, sipping afternoon tea, their heads pressed close, discussing their future marriage. They would be married right there, the ceremony on the gazebo.

Paul put his hand in front of my eyes and waving it back and forth, he said, "Mariah, where are you?"

"What?" I asked, coming slowly out of my daydream.

"What do you think of it?" he asked. "You seemed so deep in thought."

"I love it, too," I told him. "Mrs. Abbott will be crazy about it!"

Paul threw himself down on the grass, and I joined him. "Now that that project is over," he said, "how would you like to see the Indian reservations, the canyons. They're closed to the public for the summer, but I know a way in."

"I thought you'd never ask," I blurted out.

Just then my mother appeared in the clearing. "It's fantastic!" she said. "It looks like it's out of a picture book!"

Kim was right behind her. "Wow!" she exclaimed, moving toward the steps.

"Whoa!" Jim cried out. "It'll be a while before the paint is dry. So don't any of you even think of touching it!"

"Don't worry, I won't let anyone get near it," my mother promised.

I got up off of the grass. "Mom, Paul's asked me to visit the reservations and canyons with him."

"That's great," my mother said, smiling. "Only just one thing. . . ."

I held my breath. "Yes-s?"

"You'll take Kim with you."

"But—"

"No arguing," she said, her face serious now. "Kim's bored to death. Besides, I want to take the entrance exams at the college as soon as I get back so that I can line up a few night classes this year. I'll have some time to study, not having her underfoot."

"We'll be glad to take her," Paul said. "Anyhow, my friend Joe Chino will be going with us, too. He knows some caves I'm not even sure of, and he's very well informed. Sometimes in the winter he conducts tours for groups."

"It all sounds beautiful," my mother said. "I'm sure Kim and Mariah will love it. I'll make a big picnic lunch for you so you can tramp around all day."

Kim clapped her hands and jumped up and down. "Good, good! Make chicken and chocolate cake and bananas."

I wouldn't be alone with Paul after all, but maybe that was good. I had to admit I really wasn't ready to be alone with him—not just yet. I was still worried about holding a long conversation with him, still a little concerned because I'd never been with a boy alone before.

"We'll go tomorrow morning if it's okay with you," Paul said to me. "I'll call Joe tonight. He has to get permission from his grandfather anyway so that we won't be trespassing."

"Is his grandfather an Indian?" I asked.

"He sure is," Paul said. "And he's one of the most important in this area."

"That makes me feel better," my mother said. "I don't want you kids going anywhere you don't belong."

That night I wrote about it to Elaine. I tried to describe the house and I tried to describe Paul. I wrote on and on about the Abbotts' beautiful home, but when I came to Paul, I could not find the words. I felt puzzled but quickly went on to another subject.

I told her about the books I had stashed away in my closet and gave her permission to read them. I confided that I would like to write like that someday. I signed it, "See ya, Mariah Johnson," and placed a stamp on the flowered envelope. All I had to do was put it in the box out on Skipalot Road and the letter carrier would pick it up.

I was doing just that the next morning when Paul drove up in his mother's station wagon. He quickly explained that his own car was not big enough for all of us and the lunch too, and anyhow we would be traveling over dirt roads.

I'd noticed a Mark V in their driveway and I mentioned it to him. "That's my father's baby," he grinned. "I have a 280–ZX you'll love," he added, "but it's not for this trip."

I jumped in beside him and we drove down a side road that led to the back of the Abbott residence. He stopped the car right at the back gate, and we got out to help load the lunch and drinks.

My mother and Kim were coming down the brick path. "It's all here," she said. "Fried chicken, melon slices, apples, bananas, cheese cubes, potato chips, chocolate cake, and a thermos full of cold lemonade."

Jim put down his paintbrush and helped her with the goodies. "You could get lost for a week in them canyons and still not run out of food," he said, laughing.

Kim crawled into the back of the car with the lunch. The sun shone so bright, it half-blinded me when I looked back at the house and waved goodbye to Mom and Jim. As Paul drove slowly down the road, I caught myself staring at his handsome profile and quickly looked away.

Chapter 10

Paul was in high spirits. I guess showing the reservations to us was like me always dragging my relatives down to see the tide pools and watch the sandcastle contest we had each year. It was like when my grandfather had come to visit from back East and I had dragged him down to the beach at five in the morning just to watch the surfers slide in and out and over the huge, crashing waves. I wished now that I could show Paul that. I mentioned it to him as we headed for Joe Chino's house.

"Oh, I know all about that. I surf myself," Paul said. "Every summer Dad and Mom and I head for Laguna Beach."

"You're kidding!" I exclaimed. "That's where I live."

"Small world, huh?" Paul said, grinning. He reached over and grabbed my hand and the touch nearly overwhelmed me. "Yeah," Paul continued. "We rent a house there, near Surf and Sand Hotel. Dad lets his assistants run the shop and we all take off for the summer. I guess I've spent every summer of my life there, except for this one."

"But why not this one?" I asked. Here Paul had been just a few miles down the coast from where I lived, and we had never once bumped into each other!

Paul didn't have time to answer me because we were approaching Joe Chino's house. A tiny house; it couldn't have been more than two rooms. A very fat lady with a green towel wrapped around her head waved to us from the front porch.

She was clearly Indian, and she looked like she had just stepped out of a painting in the book Paul had given me. She waved again and gave us a warm smile. "He will be out in a minute," she hollered.

Out bounded a boy much shorter than Paul, his skin quite dark, but not as dark as the fat lady's. He carried a small khaki backpack over matching khaki shorts and shirt.

Joe climbed into the back seat with Kim after the proper introductions and he answered the many questions Kim started asking. We had gone about two miles when suddenly Paul turned onto a rough, bumpy dirt road.

"Now this isn't the one the tourists use," Paul pointed out as we rattled along. There were so many holes in the road, his voice shook with each vibration of the car. "The other one is a toll road at the south end of Palm Canyon Drive. You have to pay to get in, but it's really worth it because you can spend the whole day here."

"Can you camp overnight?" Kim asked.

"No," Joe answered. "There are four Indian-owned canyons surrounding Palm Springs—Andreas, Palm, Tahquitz, and Murray. Tahquitz and Palm Canyons were once sacred Indian burial grounds. Now people from all over the world come here and climb on the rocks where Indians made their homes."

Paul drove the station wagon under a cluster of palm trees which seemed permanently hemmed in by huge prickly cacti. "We can't go any further in the car. This is the secret entrance, Kim."

Joe laughed. "You make it sound mysterious, Paul. No, but there are good reasons why they just can't let the tourists in during the hot summer—fires and such. Anyway, not very many people would enjoy it. You've got to admit, it's pretty hot right now."

Joe parted the prickly bushes with a stick he'd picked up. In this area, the barbed wire fence had been torn or knocked down, leaving just enough space for us to crawl through. You'd have to know it was there because you'd never be able to see it on your own, even from the dirt road.

Joe led us past a huge towering slab of rock, and there was space for only one at a time to pass through. On the other side of the rock, Joe parted giant ferns and held them back for Kim and I gasped as we stepped into the green, huge forest.

"This is called Andreas Canyon," Joe told us, smiling with pride.

"I've never seen anything like this," I gushed.

Paul stopped beside each tree, bush and bit of foliage, naming them all. "Sycamore, alder, wild grapes, mesquite, moss, tamarisk...."

The sun peeked through the lush surroundings, making unusual feathery patterns on the spongy ground. I couldn't believe my eyes. Just seconds ago we had been in a desert, the sun beating down on us without mercy. Now we were in the middle of some kind of paradise. I just couldn't believe it!

From somewhere off in the distance I could hear the splashings of a waterfall. I looked over at Paul who was right beside me. He knew my exact thoughts.

"I'll show you the waterfall—the water is icy cold. You'll love it."

Joe and Paul picked up the bags of lunch and carried them down the narrow path they knew so well.

"A lot of people visit Palm Springs and never get beyond their motel room," Paul said. "I feel sorry for them, never to see this."

They pushed ahead and held huge branches aside for Kim and me to pass through. Finally we got to a trail made for the tourists. About one mile down the trail we found the waterfall. It was so beautiful, so majestic, I will be able to see it whenever I call on that memory again.

"If you think that's beautiful, you should see the one located at the canyon's head. Come on, let's go. I'm sure even Kim can make it!" Joe seemed to love to tease my little sister.

"I can go anywhere you guys go," Kim said bravely.

We trudged on, all of us helping to carry the lunch. After about another mile, Joe pointed out an old palm tree. "It has a legend," he told us. *"La Reina del Canyon*—the Queen of the Canyon. I guess it is probably the tallest palm in the gorge. It stands alone and the funny thing about it is, it's completely bare of the brown skirts that the other trees wear. It's a mystery, a real mystery. No one knows why it is bare and all the others are not.

"And over there—that's Gossip Rock," Joe told us. He had pointed out a huge flat boulder. "Legend has it that it was so named because Indian women used the boulder to grind out the grain for the evening meal. They'd work and talk among themselves and you can check it out for yourself. You can still see grindstone holes on that rock."

Finally we were at the canyon's head. Joe had been right; it had been worth the hike. The gush of the water over the rocks, pouring splendidly downward, sparkling in the sunlight that filtered through the many different kinds of trees was one of the most beautiful sights I'd ever seen. I'd have to describe it in one of the books that I would write someday.

"This has to be heaven," I told Paul. "Thanks for bringing us here. I love it."

He nodded and smiled. "I knew you would," he said, satisfied that he could share the beauty with someone. He looked at me for a moment and a chill went through me. We kneeled down and touched the icy water and then scooped it up in our hands. It had the most wonderful, fresh taste and I drank eagerly.

We hiked on, the cliffs forming sheer towering walls, and we passed caves where Joe told us many visitors had found pieces of history.

"This land was not only the summer home of the Agua Caliente Indians, but also their farm and grazing land," Joe told us after we'd found a good spot to eat our lunch. "There was a terrible storm one summer just before the tribe was to move back to the valley. The cloudburst washed away the rich topsoil and the crops that had been packed for the journey. Afterwards there were only huge boulders and a barren gorge."

"You said there are other canyons. Are they all like this one?" I asked.

Joe picked up his chicken leg and reached for a napkin. "They each have their own, well, I guess you can say, unique beauty. Tahquitz is closed permanently to the public now. That's because of the fear of fire in that area. It's only one and a half miles from the center of the town. That's where the movie *Lost Horizon* was made. The waterfall you see in that movie is the same one in that canyon."

"It's a sixty-foot drop over sheer granite," Paul added. "Now that's a fall I wouldn't want to take."

No one talked for a while, we were so busy eating.

"Your mom's a good cook," Joe said, finishing off another chicken leg.

"Thanks," Kim said. "Now we don't have to carry so much back," she laughed, watching Paul take his second banana.

"Hiking sure makes you hungry," I added.

"Now if we were in Murray Canyon, we could show you some wild ponies, maybe," Joe told us.

"Really wild . . . they don't belong to anyone?" Kim asked, wiping off her mouth.

"We think they're descendants of horses belonging to the early Indians," Joe said.

"Wow!" Kim said in wonder, brushing off her jeans as she stood up.

"Do you know that people have dug up weapons and utensils around the Indian campsites that date back ten thousand years?" Joe said, standing.

"And there are naturally hot mineral springs," Paul added as we began to clean up our lunch.

"And when does this place officially open to the public?" I asked Joe.

"Sometime in October," he answered. "It's all up to how dry the weather has been. Our greatest fear here is always fire. Perhaps it was to those Indians as well."

"Palm Canyon, what's that like?" I asked.

"It's fabulous for taking photographs," Paul said. "I mean, people come from everywhere to do just that. There are about three thousand wild desert fan palms on the canyon's edge. It's really beautiful. And then you hike on the trail down to the canyon floor where there are warm mineral springs bubbling out of the ground."

"I could really get my toes into that," I said with a laugh. "Can we go there today?"

"No," Paul said. "It's best to visit just one a day . . . if that's okay with you," he added.

"Fine," I told him. "We've got the rest of the summer."

"Well, I won't really have that much time," Paul told me, helping me climb over a jagged rock. "I'm scheduled to go into the hospital next Monday. I've been putting it off for a while." His face suddenly looked as if an unpleasant memory had crossed his mind.

We were standing on another rock further down from the falls. It wasn't as big as Gossip Rock, but it was big enough for several people. Looking around I saw that we had come into somewhat of a circle. Paul's entrance to the place was just a short distance from the rock we were standing on.

Paul sat down and I decided to join him. Joe shouted back at us, "I'm going to show Kim the cave I found last summer. Are you coming?"

"Not just right now," Paul said. "We'll catch up in a minute."

The sun filtered through the empty spaces between the huge trees and made beautiful lacy patterns of light on the rock. "Why the hospital?" I asked lightly, hoping I wasn't being too nosy. What if the question had been something a girl shouldn't ask a guy, I wondered, sorry I had asked. But before I had too much time to worry about it, he was telling me.

"No big deal," he said, taking off his tennis shoes. His toes were long and slender. I pulled off my shoes and together we held out our feet, comparing them.

"They're huge boats," I said, meaning my own feet.

"Then what are mine, aircraft carriers?" He laughed. It felt good to be barefoot. Paul was smiling now.

"Your toes are fat and pudgy," he told me. "It looks like you were running too fast and smashed into a stone wall."

I picked up my shoe and hit him on the head. "Hey," he backed away and laughed and then we both laughed together. "C'mon. Feet *are* silly looking when you think of it," he said, chuckling.

And then, without warning, he went back to the original subject. "I've had two cysts removed already," he said quietly. "They're like little lumps—tumors—and they grow right under the skin. I had one removed from the back of my ear last winter," he said, pointing to his right ear. "And then one from under my left arm."

"Oh," I said. "That's terrible. Was it very painful?"

"The cyst or the operation? The cyst doesn't hurt at all. It's like a lump, but it grows. It starts out like a little hard seed and then it gets like the size of a pea. The doctor measures it each time you go to his office and then he decides if he really should remove it. As far as the operation goes, you don't feel anything until after the anesthesia wears off. See this little scar right in back of my jaw?"

I looked and found the little jagged line. "It's really not much now, but last year it looked red and ugly and I thought it would be there for life. Now you have to really look to find it."

"And now, this operation?" I asked, gingerly. I sounded terrible.

"Under my arm—my right arm this time. I'll go in Monday and come home possibly the next day. No big deal," he said. "I had a terrible argument with my mother about it; the scheduling. It seemed so unfair to me. It took away our Laguna vacation. It seemed we could have waited."

"But isn't it important to get it done now?" I shuddered. Lumps, cysts—I'd heard those words associated with cancer.

Paul must have seen the horrified look on my face.

"Really, it's nothing. It's not serious at all." And then he changed the conversation completely. "Your name, Mariah. How did you get it? It's so unusual."

"You don't like it?" I asked defensively.

"No, no." Paul laughed. "I like it, but it's so different. How do you spell it?"

I spelled it out slowly, wondering if he was laughing at me. "When my mother was pregnant with me, my father was working in insurance. But his first love was our little local theater where they'd put on plays and musicals. He loved it so much, it was hard to tear him away, my mother told me. He was doing *Paint Your Wagon* on the night I was born. My father missed the whole thing. He always laughed about that and said it was far more important for my mother to be present.

"Anyhow," I went on, "my father sang in the men's chorus, and one song was "They Call

The Wind Maria," but they pronounced it like my name sounds—Mariah. My father loved that song and so when he finally got to the hospital he asked my mother to call me Mariah. They changed the spelling so that people would not call me Maria by mistake."

Paul didn't speak for a while and then, "It sounds to me like your father must be a very interesting guy."

"Oh, he is," I said, happy that Paul had given me an opportunity to talk about him. "He's terribly good-looking, too, and talented."

"Couldn't he come to Palm Springs?"

It always came back to that. No matter what the conversation was with people, I always had to confess that my parents were divorced.

"No," I told him, putting my shoes back on. "The day I was fourteen, he left us." I might as well tell him everything and get it over with, I thought. "He ran off with a woman from his office. They flew to a small town near Chicago, her hometown, and my father got a job in Chicago selling air conditioners."

"Are they still together?"

"No, and that's a funny thing. Just the other day, I went to my mother's bedroom to pick up her scarf. A letter from my father was on the bed. I thought it was a recent one and I grabbed it and scanned it. And then I finally looked at the date—way back in January sometime. I know now that that little romance lasted a very short while, and all this time my father has been asking to come back!"

"And your mother won't let him?"

"She's too proud, I guess. And Paul, I'm only guessing. Why she had that old letter out, I'll never know, but she must have been reading it again. He begged her to let him come back. He said he wanted to be a good father and husband. He wanted a second chance. Maybe she's considering it." I was surprised at myself for confiding in Paul like this. But I felt so comfortable with him, I just let the words come out.

We sat in silence for a while, Paul looking thoughtful, as though he was wondering about the letter too. And then he broke it. "I guess you have a lot of friends back in Laguna. I mean, you must be pretty popular," he said, shifting his position on the rock.

A sudden terror went through me. How could I tell him that I'd never had a date—a real date? Anyhow, why should I ruin my chances with him by letting him know I wasn't popular at all?

My mind raced. "Rob," I blurted out.

"What?" he asked.

"Well, of course, I have a lot of friends. I mean, you know, like you have, but then there's Rob. In the last year and a half I've been dating him pretty heavily."

It was too late. My imagination had the best of me. The only thing I could do was just keep talking, and maybe, later on, he'd forget the details.

"Yes, Rob Anderson," I told him, trying not to blush. "He's, well, I guess he's about one or two inches taller than you and he has...very dark hair and dark, dark eyes...and he's...a football player...he's a quarterback."

"Oh. Then he's a pretty big man there?" Paul said slowly.

"Oh, yes. The biggest," I lied. "Mostly we go to the movies and stuff like that."

"I keep pretty busy myself," Paul said, looking up at the sun peeking through the branches. "Yeah, pretty busy. Jean...she likes to go to the movies too. A real movie buff. She was a cheerleader, too. I guess you could say she's the best. She's going to Berkeley, too."

My heart turned over in my chest like a pancake doing a somersault. "Jean?" I asked weakly. Of course, what a fool I was. With Paul's good looks, there had to be someone, maybe a lot of someones. Now I knew how he spent his nights.

"She has long, blond, wavy hair," he continued and I wasn't sure I wanted to hear it. "And her skin, it's so perfect she never even uses makeup—except a light lipstick."

A goddess! I wondered if we should tell Hollywood, I thought sarcastically.

"And she has the prettiest laugh," he continued. "Like, well, when she laughs it's like—"

"Like the tinkling of two crystal glasses touching?" I asked, feeling a little mean.

He gave me a puzzled look and then we both started to laugh. But inside, I wasn't laughing. Inside I was moaning. I finally had attracted someone and now I'd found that he was already taken! And by no less than a potential movie star.

We sat silently for about three or four minutes more and then I could hear my sister far off in the distance. She was shouting something about a "piece of history" they had found. Joe's words, I was sure.

"Before they come back," Paul said in a whisper, "I want to tell you about this rock. This is my rock. Joe doesn't even know it. I'm really supposed to have him with me if I sneak into the reservations in the summer, but I come here whenever I have to think things out."

I smiled warmly at Paul. He had his rock also! "You're laughing at me," he said, frowning.

"No, no," I told him, reaching out and touching his arm. "Someday I'll show you my rock, the one where I go to sit and think." And then we both broke out into great peals of laughter.

Kim was below Paul's rock now, holding out a piece of stone. "Look, look," she called up to us. "Joe says this is a real arrowhead!"

It looked just like any stone to me, but I'd take Joe's word for it. Paul helped me off the great boulder, his hand felt warm and rough in mine. Then we started down the trail home. I stopped for a moment and looked back at Paul's rock. I could see where Paul's feet had trampled down the weeds surrounding the rock, where he could get a foothold in one of the slabs to pull himself up.

He must come here often, I thought. To

think, Paul was a lot like me. I thought again of Jean, and wondered if she knew about Paul's rock. Whether Paul had taken her here also. Well, easy come, easy go, and laughing again to myself I turned back to the path and walked away. Jean or no Jean, Paul was a friend.

I had no way of knowing that day, that the next time I saw that rock, my laughter would have turned into tears.

Chapter 11

Right after breakfast the next morning, the phone rang. "How would you like to go down to the book shop with me this morning, help me stock some books for Dad?"

"Sure. Let me see if it's okay with my mother," I told him.

Mom was in her bedroom making up the bed and when I asked her if she needed me she said she didn't. And then, as I was leaving the room, she said, "Mariah, you like Paul very much, don't you?"

"I guess it shows," I told her, my face and neck quickly catching on fire. I hadn't really admitted it out loud to anyone before.

She came over to me and pushed a few stray hairs away from my cheek. "Go slow," she said softly. "You have a whole lifetime ahead of you."

I knew exactly what she meant. She was trying to tell me not to push my relationship with Paul. Not to get involved too heavy, too fast. I understood. Why then was there this terrible urgency in me to run, to hurry, to establish our friendship, to seal with him some kind of bond between us?

"I'll be okay," I told her. "I left him hanging

on the phone. I'd better run back or he'll think I forgot him." What a stupid thing to say, I thought. How could I ever forget him?

"I'll be ready in about thirty minutes," I told him, out of breath.

"See ya," he said and hung up.

Paul picked me up in his silver 280-ZX. "I love it," I told him, sinking down into the red leather seat. I guess money comes in handy sometimes."

"My dad didn't just hand it to me," Paul said as we drove down Skipalot Drive, turned down another, and headed for downtown. "Ever since I was a little kid, I've helped him in the store. I've done plenty of odd jobs for the Abbotts, too. My dad never paid me. He gave me spending money only when I was desperate. But on graduation day, he gave me a little silver box. I thought it was a watch, but there they were, the keys to this baby." His pride was evident.

"Very classy," I said, feeling the red leather. "I've never been in anything like this before."

"Jean loves it, too," he said suddenly. It was like a bucket of cold water had been thrown in my face.

"Yeah," I said, quickly composing myself, "all Rob has is an old Chevy, but it gets us around."

In what seemed like seconds we were in front of the book shop, searching for a parking place. We circled once around the block, then on our second pass, we saw a white car pulling out of a space.

"We're in luck," Paul said as he swung the silver car into the slot.

The book shop was like nothing I'd ever seen before. All the shelves were organized neatly, and a sign welcomed the customers to the lounge in the back of the store to sit and read, or just relax. A silver coffeepot on a silver tray welcomed customers to have a cup. On another table was a pitcher of iced tea and frosted glasses. Two light brown leather sofas were arranged in front of a glowing fireplace, and because the shop was air-conditioned, the heat from the fireplace was comfortable. Sprinkled throughout the room were other leather reclining chairs and footstools.

"How nice, how comfortable and inviting," I told Paul, and then I saw him wave to a lady behind the counter. He waited until she was finished with her customer and then he slipped behind the counter and touched her hand, drawing her over to me.

"Mom, this is Mariah Johnson. Mariah, my mother."

He must have told her about me, I thought. Otherwise, he would have followed my name with an explanation, like "the girl over at the Abbotts'." Mrs. Strobe smiled dutifully at me, her mouth somewhat stiff. She was so much older than I thought she would be. In her fifties, I would guess.

I extended my hand, but she took it reluctantly and dropped it quickly. I could feel a hot blush dotting my cheeks. Paul ignored my discomfort and his mother's bad manners and turned to her. "Would you care if I showed Mariah around?"

Mrs. Strobe turned and greeted a customer by her first name, and then turned back to me. She was addressing Paul, but she was looking straight at me. "Of course you may, Paul but please don't forget your doctor's appointment this afternoon. He wants to take some more blood for the tests before Monday."

Paul's hand flew to his forehead and he cupped it over his eyes. "Oh, God! I *did* forget." And then he turned to me. "I wanted to spend the whole day with you, but we'll have to be heading home right after lunch. Mariah, I'm sorry."

And I knew he was, but his mother, that was another story. I could tell she was very pleased that Paul had to break our date. Why couldn't she be pleasant, I wondered.

Paul then introduced me to his father. Mr. Strobe had gray hair, heavy dark-rimmed glasses, and a nice smile. He put his hands over mine and held them warmly for a moment.

"Paul has told us about your family," Mr. Strobe said, his dark brown eyes shining behind the glasses. His nose was like Paul's, as was his smile. I liked his father and I got the definite feeling he liked me, too.

After the formalities were over, Paul took me to the stockroom and explained the intricate system of inventory, stocking, special sales, and promotions.

"We own a bookstore in Laguna Beach,

too," he said and I stepped away from Paul in delightful surprise.

"You do? Which one?"

"The Book Notch. Near the ocean."

I smiled. I'd spent countless hours there.

"Yes, that's why we go there in the summer. It gives my parents a chance to check over the management and keep on top of the operation and still enjoy the ocean."

I was helping him stick tiny price stickers on the corners of a stack of Betty Crocker cookbooks. "Why did your folks let one tiny operation spoil your whole summer, Paul? In fact, you could have had it done in some hospital near Laguna and then—"

"Because the doctor they have so much faith in practices here," Paul explained. "Also when I questioned it some time ago, Dad said he's always wanted to spend the summer here in Palm Springs to actually see what goes on with the summer tourists. He makes friends of all of his customers and he says he has missed out on not knowing some of the summer people."

My question had been a nosy one, one I should not have asked, but the answer had been unsatisfying to me. I had a strange and uneasy feeling that there was more to it all than I knew. Yet, at the same time, I knew Paul wasn't lying to me.

We finished pricing the cookbooks and moved on to a series of books on car repairs. Paul handed me a fat book on Mustangs and it slipped from my hand. We both reached down for it and bumped heads, our laughter mingling with the pain of it. And then, suddenly Paul reached out and held my face in both of his hands. At first his lips on mine felt like the touch of a feather. Then we were both drawing away from each other with the surprise of it all, and then coming together again, the kiss this time no longer questioning, but sure of itself. Our bodies did not touch. Our arms did not reach out and encircle each other. Only our lips met for a split second and then broke away.

The book on Mustangs still lay on the floor, and Paul bent down and picked it up. My body trembled still from the kiss, and when I looked at Paul stacking the book among the others, I saw his hand shake, too. Neither of us said another word until all the books were in order.

"I know a great place up the street that makes terrific sandwiches," Paul offered. "What do you think, Mariah?" He seemed to want to change the mood.

"Sounds good to me," I said, my voice shaking slightly with the newness of my first kiss. I turned to go and realized my knees felt like they had turned to water. I hoped Paul hadn't noticed.

We waved goodbye to the Strobes as we left the busy book shop. Paul led me by the hand to his car and all the while I could feel his mother's eyes on me. Mingled with a feeling that made me want to skip down the street was a feeling that something was wrong.

Instead of stopping for lunch, though, Paul abruptly headed the car in the direction of Skipalot Drive.

"Where are we going?" I asked.

"Thought I'd better take you home."

"Oh," I said, slightly uneasy. Then looking out the window, I noticed a group of girls outside a restaurant, the one Paul probably meant. Now it made sense. One of those girls must be Jean and Paul doesn't want her to see me. Maybe I'm winning out over her. A feeling of smug satisfaction came over me.

We were almost home when Paul mentioned his mother. "She doesn't have to work in the store like she does," he said, "but she likes to keep busy and she loves books and people."

I'm people, I thought. Why doesn't she like me? But I didn't mention it to Paul. I didn't think he'd want to talk about it now.

He drove around to the Abbotts' back gate and jumped out, swiftly running around to my side of the car to open my door. Paul evidently had been taught all the nice things, the proper things when with the opposite sex. He did them all with ease. I wondered what his mother would think if she knew he knew how to kiss with ease.

We stopped at the gazebo. "It's dry now," Paul said, putting his hand out to lead me up the two steps. It seemed we were the couple in my daydream. Paul slipped his arm around my shoulder and he and I just sat there for the longest time, quietly enjoying the moment. I thought of Jean. Was he comparing our kiss to those he had shared with her?

"Is something wrong?" he asked.

"No," I lied. "Paul, how long will you be in the hospital?"

"Just a few days—two at the very most," he answered. "Then there will be tests. I'll have several after the operation, if it's like last time."

We sat closer together, my hair touching his. I could feel his warm breath on my cheek. If I turned my face just slightly, my lips would meet his again. How foolish I had been to worry so about a first kiss. So many times I'd sat and wondered how it would be. Would I do it right? How would I know exactly how? With Paul it had been so natural, his mouth had fit perfectly on mine. For a fraction of a second I had feared he would laugh at the trembling of my lips, but then I had been delighted that his trembled too.

I turned my face and Paul kissed me again. A long, long lasting kiss and then we sat together in the afternoon sun in that beautiful gazebo enjoying the closeness and pleasure of just being together.

Suddenly Paul jumped up and looked at his watch. "What's wrong with me? I almost forgot again!" Turning to me, he said, "Mariah, I've got to run."

He was out of the gazebo in a flash. "See you later," he called to me, and I watched as he disappeared out the back gate. His kiss was still warm on my lips.

Chapter 12

The morning Paul entered the hospital looked the same as every summer morning in Palm Springs. The birds got up early after a restless night to start their chorus, and the sun popped out of the fluffy white clouds looking like a round gold coin that had just been cleaned with polish.

From the west wing of the house I could peer out of one of the upstairs windows and see Paul getting into his father's copper-colored Mark V. I could see a good part of his house, too.

It was a one-story, strictly modern house that rambled all over the place, but the most fantastic thing about it was the pool. It was perfectly round, which is no big thing, but right out in the middle of it, stood a round slab and on it a table with four wrought iron chairs. To get to the slab, you had to swim or use a wooden footbridge, like the kind that you see in Japanese gardens.

I watched Mrs. Strobe come out of the house then. If she just looked up, she would catch me spying, I thought, but luckily she did not. I thought how much his folks looked like grandparents—they were so much older than my own. Jim had filled me in on that one: "The Strobes wanted a child for so long, and they'd been told by doctors that there wouldn't be any. And then it happened, when Mrs. Strobe was thirty-nine and her husband a year older. They were so happy you'd a-thought they were going to bust with it!"

Mr. Strobe followed closely behind his wife. Dressed in a dark blue business suit, he looked like a banker. Mrs. Strobe was wearing a pretty blue, silky-looking dress, and her hair framed her face beautifully. Paul had told me that she had dyed it brown up until last year, when his father finally broke down and told her that he really loved gray hair on her. So now she kept it that way. She made a stunning figure beside her husband.

Paul had explained to me on the phone the night before that the operation had been pushed up to Tuesday morning because they had scheduled more tests for him all day Monday.

"I think I lack iron or something in my blood," he had informed me. "No big thing." And then he had added that he would be home on Wednesday afternoon—if everything went well. I hoped he was right about it being "no big thing."

My mother entered the bedroom. "There you are, Mariah." She joined me at the window. "Well, there they go," she said, her shoulder touching mine.

"Mom, Paul said he'd be home Wednesday afternoon if everything *went well.* What do you think he meant?" I asked.

"Lumps like that can be malignant," she

answered. "Cancer. Lots of times when they discover cancer, though, they can start different procedures and treatments that will stop it from spreading to the rest of the body."

That's why they didn't want to wait, I thought, and then I turned my face from the view of the car slowly pulling away from the house. "Mom, do you think—do you think Paul could have cancer?" My voice was so soft a whisper that my mouth barely moved when I formed the words.

"Not necessarily. Some people seem to be prone to have little lumps or tumors, Mariah. Remember your Great-Aunt Helen? She must have had ten removed from all parts of her body and none, absolutely none, were malignant. Maybe Paul's like her. He looks like a very healthy young man, even though I'd say he's too thin. I doubt that there is any real trouble. The Strobes have an awful lot of money, and people like that can spend plenty on tests and more tests. Remember, Paul is their only child."

"And so, it will all be okay," I said, leaving the window, heading for my own bedroom. "I mean, if it is something, the Strobes have plenty of money to fix him up." My thoughts wouldn't go further.

My mother gave me a strange look, opened up her mouth to say something, but then just gave me a peck on the cheek. "Hurry cleaning up your room, Mariah. I need you to help me polish the silverware this morning—and there's plenty of it."

We left the bedroom. Plenty of money, I had

said to my mother. What if plenty of money wasn't enough? What if all the money in the whole world wouldn't be able to help Paul? I wondered if he were as scared as I was.

I walked into Mr. Abbott's library and scanning the titles I finally found what I was looking for. Turning the pages of the medical encyclopedia, I stopped when I got to the section on cancer. I hadn't realized there were so many different kinds. I breathed a little easier after I read the section that said that in many cases cancer could be cured completely. If the worst was true and what Paul had was cancer, the doctors would be able to give him drugs and eliminate it. The treatment could be painful though, and I prayed Paul wouldn't have to go through anything like that.

The rest of the day was spent helping my mother in the kitchen. We polished all of the Abbotts' silver together, but I might have been on another planet for all the conversation we *didn't* have. I polished the forks. I hated to do forks, especially since you had to make sure you got inside of all the tines. I got the funny feeling that my mother had purposely given me them—to keep my mind off of Paul.

"I'd like to visit him," I said, placing the last fork in its dark maroon velvet sack.

"You can't," my mother said. "They just don't want anyone around."

"How do you know?" I asked, surprised.

"I talked with Mrs. Strobe on the phone. She called here that day you were all at the

94

Indian reservation. She was upset that Paul had gone when she had specifically asked him not to."

"I didn't know that. He hadn't mentioned it," I said, my feeling of surprise turning to annoyance. Mrs. Strobe treated Paul like a small child!

My mother finished packing the little maroon sacks in the huge wooden box that held the entire set of silver. "I can't figure the woman out," she exclaimed. "She's never met me, yet I get the feeling that she doesn't like me. Just listening to her voice. She told me—or I should say announced—that Paul was scheduled for this operation and that she had wanted him to get lots of rest beforehand. I told her that if we'd known about that, we would have certainly kept you all home."

"But what did she say about the hospital?"

"It's funny. I didn't even mention it. She came right out with it herself. She said that if we were thinking of visiting her son, we should think twice. First of all, the time would be spent with numerous blood tests and so forth. And then following the operation she didn't think he would be quite up to it. She did say perhaps Paul could receive visitors after he came home."

I smiled. Receive visitors. "Sounds like you have to have a name card to get past the butler." Secretly I was glad to have an ally.

"Don't be nasty," my mother said. "The woman is obviously very upset about her son

95

entering the hospital. Paul is their only child, and they're almost fanatical in overprotecting him."

That Thursday I received a letter from Elaine. I read it several times, just to fill in time until Paul came home.

Dear Mariah,

I love your house. We all do—even the boys. My mom wants me to add, she is being very careful that they behave and do not hurt anything in your lovely home. At first I couldn't sleep because of the waves and all, but now they seem to lull me to sleep. Our whole family goes down to the beach every day where we found the most interesting tide pools not too far from your house. You must know the spots. The boys love the pools and poke around them for hours. We found several starfish washed up with the seaweed and the boys brought one in the house and hid it in the closet. I think they planned to take it back home and put it on their bedroom wall, but things didn't turn out. It took my mom several days to find out what the horrible smell was. Anyhow, it is all okay now because she sprayed everything with Lysol.

We're going to cook hot dogs down on the beach tonight, so I better go now. Before I do, I must tell you that I did start to read some of those books. I especially liked the one about the girl who is trying to find out about her husband's family secret and she is up in the attic and her sister-in-law walks in and tries to kill her. Don't tell me what happens.

Always,
Elaine Gretel

P.S. Paul Strobe sounds great. Are you telling me everything?

I sat on the window seat and watched the sun set and then the darkness settle in around the lacy woodwork on the ivory gazebo. All I could think of was Paul. Once in a while the name "Jean" reared its ugly head, and I pushed it, or tried to push it, out of my thoughts. Maybe Jean was visiting him in the hospital. Maybe Jean was rich, too, and that's why Mrs. Strobe didn't like me running around with Paul. Wouldn't she want only the very best for her rich son?

When I brushed my teeth that night, I said to the girl in the mirror, through toothpaste and all, "Disgusting! She can't be thinking that—that's so narrow-minded!"

The girl with the foamy mouth laughed back at me. "Oh, yeah?" she said, and I groaned and scrubbed even harder.

Later that night, I picked up my pen and started the letter I owed Elaine.

How are you and my house so far? Did you get to Laguna and see all the neat shops? Do you surf yourself, or do you just watch them like I do? If you like to fish, you might drive over to the pier in Huntington Beach. That city also has the greatest library around, in my opinion. Also don't miss visiting the Queen Mary in Long Beach. I sound like a travel agency or a television commercial. I ought to get a commission.

And then I ended the letter with:

On top of my white chest of drawers you will find a jewelry box my father made for me when I was three. Inside is an Easter egg that Kim blew out last year and then painted it blue and dotted it with tiny, silver stars. It looks just like the sky here, just before dark.

Well, anyhow, the blue—that's the exact, I mean the exact color of Paul's eyes. I mean it. Now isn't that something?

That night I wrote in my notebook: "When we stand together, my head just comes up to his shoulders. He has nice hands. When he helped me climb his rock, he held his hand out to me and I took it. It felt warm and strong and I had the funny feeling that as long as I held onto his hand, I would never fall."

Chapter 13

They brought Paul home on Friday afternoon. He had been in the hospital five days. Not two like he'd said.

I couldn't stand it any longer! "I'm calling the house," I told my mother. "Just to see how it went!"

She gave a long sigh and then said, "Okay. I don't see why not. Better to call and be insulted by Mrs. Strobe than have Paul think we don't care about him."

I was delighted when Paul answered the phone himself. He sounded great, like the Paul I knew. "Hey," he shouted through the phone, "everything went terrific! No problem. I've got my arm in a sling like I told you I would, but nothing really hurts."

I felt like jumping up and down and shouting it out to the world. Paul was okay! He was really okay! He didn't have cancer after all!

"I want you to come over for a while," he went on. "Let's see. . . . I'm supposed to take a quick nap and then . . . how about around seven tonight?"

A chill circled my neck and my face grew hot at the same time. He was asking me to come over, not Jean. Maybe he'd seen enough of Jean while he was in the hospital. Maybe he was just asking me to anger his mother. I didn't care what the reason; I was going.

I brushed my hair until it had to shine or fall out. I chose my blue silk blouse and my dark blue pants with the gold belt, and after checking the full-length mirror in my bedroom, I pulled them off and put on the salmon-colored blouse and the dark brown pants. Then after I'd yanked them off, I settled on my brown and orange check shirt and a clean pair of jeans. Slowly I descended the staircase, but when I was halfway down, I ran back and changed into my blue outfit again.

All of this activity left me all sweaty, and if my mother hadn't stopped me and told me it was getting late, I probably would have undressed and showered again.

"You must go bearing gifts," my mother said, handing me the chocolate cake she had baked after my phone call to Paul. I could see its lemon frosting through the plastic container.

"Um-m," I said. "Mom, thank you, thanks so much for your trouble." And then, "Wait a minute," I told her, handing back the cake. I raced back up the stairs toward my stack of books. Quickly I selected one. I wanted to tell Paul about my writing, the kind of writing I wanted to do, and to understand this, I felt he should read one of these books.

There was one that described a big whaling ship in detail. That was the one where an English lord drags off one of the slave girls. He could skip that part if he didn't like it, but he'd love the whaling part. I tucked it under my arm and then racing down the stairs I grabbed the cake from my mother. "I'm on my way," I yelled to her, heading for the door.

"Thank God," my mother said, and her dimples showed when she smiled.

Mrs. Strobe came to the front door herself, responding to the elaborate sound of chimes and then more chimes. I stood back, surprised—I had pushed the button only once. I'd never heard such a doorbell.

She stood there, looking very stately, but with a surprised look in her faded blue eyes. "Yes-s?" she said, ending the word with a question mark.

"Paul—Paul invited me over," I stuttered sheepishly, thrusting the cake in her face. Mrs. Strobe's eyes grew wider and she appeared to be backing away from me.

"Oh-h?" she said, her voice sliding to a higher key.

Then from behind the half-opened door, Mr. Strobe appeared. "Welcome, welcome, Mariah! Good to see you again," he said in a loud, booming voice.

I lowered the cake that I had held out in front of me and he quickly stepped around his wife and took it.

"What a wonderful surprise!" he boomed.

"Didn't Paul tell you I was coming?" I stammered. "I guess I thought he would have told you."

Mr. Strobe laughed and placed the cake on

a glass-topped table in the entrance hall. He held out his hands and took mine. "We had no idea, but we're so happy to see you. It must mean that Paul is feeling better."

Paul entered the hall then, and I shuddered. He looked so pale and thin! Since I had seen him last, he must have dropped at least four or five pounds. He smiled a broad smile, though, and his blue eyes shone as he held out his hand to me. It closed over mine, and even in front of his mother and father he would not let it go.

"Thanks for coming," he said, looking straight at me. "I was dying of boredom. We can play backgammon or maybe just sit and listen to some of my tapes."

Mrs. Strobe led us into a gigantic formal living room. Everything was done in Oriental style—vases, mahogany tables in all sizes, display cabinets with statues inside them, Japanese dolls. I had never seen anything so beautiful. Then we walked down three thickly carpeted stairs into what seemed like a massive garden room. It was still inside the house, but it was like an outside garden with a glass ceiling. Huge plants stood everywhere and aquariums filled with beautifully colored fish lined the walls.

"This is our orchid room," Mrs. Strobe said proudly, pointing out hundreds of orchids in different colors. If I could have picked out one flower for Mrs. Strobe, it would have been the orchid. They're both so proper, so cold, so snobbish, and rich.

In one corner stood a stone fireplace, the

largest I'd ever seen. On its mantle were many pictures, most of them of Paul. The photos were lined up from when he was an infant to where he was right now. I loved them. Mrs. Strobe smiled at my approval.

From out of nowhere, Nellie, the maid, appeared. Mr. Strobe instructed her to serve the cake, which was still in the vestibule. In a few minutes she returned, carrying the cake on a lovely silver-trimmed tray.

She offered coffee or tea and we all chose coffee. There were real linen napkins on the tray bound in silver rings, and the fork I picked up almost blinded me with its shine. I could appreciate Nellie's good work on that silver.

We were all seated on rattan furniture, Mr. Strobe on a comfortable armchair and Paul and I on a love seat. Mrs. Strobe sat back on a wide-backed "Queen" chair and somehow the conversation turned to the Indian reservations.

Mr. Strobe talked for some time about the history of the Indians and the community of Palm Springs. He told me about a man named Judge John Guthrie McCallum, a San Francisco attorney, and how the man had come to the area way back in 1884. The judge had first learned of the place from an Indian guide and an interpreter, Bill Pablo. At the time they were living in San Bernardino, where they had moved in the hope of saving their son's life.

"What was wrong with their son?" I asked.

"During the typhoid epidemic in 1879, John, his son, became ill," Mr. Strobe went on. "It seemed the wise thing to do to move to a dry, hot climate and so that is how Judge McCallum became the first white resident to make Palm Springs his home."

"The library downtown is named after some-body," I said, hoping I didn't sound too stupid. "Why didn't they name it after him?"

"A good observation," Mr. Strobe answered. "After McCallum moved here, he persuaded an eccentric Scotsman named Welwood Murray to move here, too. He and his lovely wife started up the very first hotel—The Palm Springs Hotel. Later the library was named in his memory."

"And you know what he did?" Paul added, laughing, "He hired an Indian, dressed him in an Arab costume, and had him meet the trains at Seven Palms on camelback. There he handed out pamphlets on Palm Valley and The Palm Springs Hotel."

"There's such a fascinating history here," Mr. Strobe added.

"I'd like to take Mariah up on the tram," Paul said to his mother.

Mrs. Strobe hadn't said a word since I came in. She quickly turned to her son, her coffee cup in midair. "Paul, you must not go running around. You've just had that operation and I promised the doctors—"

"Of course," I interrupted her. Then I turned to Paul beside me. "You've got to listen to her. She knows best." I had read the concern for Paul in Mrs. Strobe's eyes. She seemed to be trying to tell me something. My interruption caused her to sit back on her chair, but I relaxed when I read a "thank you" in her troubled eyes.

"But I feel great," Paul protested, getting up and taking great strides around the room. "The summer is flying by. Pretty soon it'll all be over and before you know, it'll be time for me to leave. Mariah will be going back home and—"

It was Mrs. Strobe's turn to interrupt. "You really must forgive my son," she said, looking directly at me. "Although the operation went well, it'll take time for him to regain his strength. His future health may depend on it."

"Here—here," Mr. Strobe protested, putting up his hand to stop the discussion. "I'm sure Paul will do the right thing. Mariah didn't come over here to listen to our babying Paul, Betty. Why don't we leave them alone for a while?"

Nellie came in and cleared the dishes. The Strobes excused themselves, Mr. Strobe mentioning that they wanted to see a television special and they would be in the den.

"Come on, Mariah. I'll beat you in backgammon," Paul said, grabbing me by the hand.

Paul's bedroom was lined with books and stereo equipment. He put on some tapes and ushered me to a corner of the room that was reserved just for backgammon.

When I saw it, I panicked. "It looks like you spend hours on the game," I said. "And you expect me to be your opponent?"

He laughed as he withdrew his pieces from the carefully stacked pile and handed me the reds. The music was soft, and his hands bumped into mine when we both reached for the dice at the same time. Without getting up, he leaned over the table and kissed my cheek, brushing my lips for an instant.

"I'd thought I dreamed it," he said, pulling away and smiling. "All the time in the hospital I'd thought I'd dreamed you up and that when I finally got home I would realize it. But you're here and everything is going to be okay with me, too." His eyes shone brightly.

"Paul, don't fight your mother," I said. I meant it.

"But we have so much to do!"

"There's plenty of time left, Paul. And even if I don't get to go up on the tram, I can always come back. I can drive here, you know."

"But I'll be up at Berkeley."

"There will be vacations."

He left his side of the board and came over to the leather chair where I sat. "You'll save them for me? But what about this Rob?"

I gasped, putting my hand over my mouth. Rob. I'd forgotten about him. "Oh, he was nothing," I finally admitted. "Really nothing."

Paul looked hurt and confused. "Hey, you can't just call a guy *nothing*. I mean, you spent a lot of time with him. You owe him an explanation, you know!"

"Wait a minute, Paul," I said, my anger and jealousy surfacing. "What about Jean? How can you sit here and kiss me and ask me to spend all my vacations with you? Are you just going to walk off and forget her?"

We both looked at each other angrily. Our

first real fight! And then after a long silence, Paul spoke. "Mariah, I want to tell you—"

"Wait," I told him. "Look, I'm sorry, Paul, but I had to do it. I couldn't let you think I wasn't popular, that I'd never had a boyfriend, never even been kissed. I—I made Rob up."

I turned my head away in shame. A ripple of laughter escaped Paul's mouth. Then he was roaring loudly, throwing his head back in great, thunderous peals of laughter.

"What-t?" I said. "I know it's funny. I know I made a fool out of myself, but I wish you wouldn't enjoy it so much!" My anger and hurt were showing, but I didn't care.

He tried to talk through his laughter, but for a few seconds could not. And then, I could hear broken sentences, mingled with laughter again. "It's—it's just that—that Jean isn't real either—I made her up for the same reason!"

At first I felt furious. How could he have deceived me like that? Then I thought of my own deception and I began to laugh, too. Together we laughed up a storm, my stomach hurting from it. Then in an instant we stopped, and I was in Paul's arms.

He held me close to him and I could feel his heart beat rapidly. "Mariah," he breathed into my hair. "No more games for us, Mariah. Let's not play any more games with each other. No more lies. We don't need them. I love you for just what you are—just you—and I think you love me in the same way."

"Oh, I do," I hissed, hugging him close.

He kissed me once more. "I'll walk you

home," he said. "Whether my mother likes it or not."

I didn't want him to overexert himself, but just as important—I didn't really want to leave him.

We walked slowly through the star-studded night. I wished the acre of land between his house and the Abbotts' had been a mile.

"I left you something in your bedroom," I told him. "It's a book—I want to write just like that. Maybe if you read it, at least scan it, you will get some idea...."

Paul stopped in his tracks. "I didn't know you wanted to write. You never told me."

"It's part of me you should know about," I said seriously.

"How long have you been writing?"

"Well, right after my kindergarten teacher showed me how to put letters together it started. I mean, I wanted to, was anxious to get started, but I guess wanting to and actually doing it.... I'd say I've really been doing it for only about two years now."

"And what kind of books?"

"The one I gave you is a Gothic. I'm pretty crazy about them."

We had reached the back gate of the Abbotts' house. "I'll tell you a secret," Paul said. "If you promise you won't tell anyone."

We headed for the gazebo. It was so romantic looking, with the full moon shining down on the two little steps. "I promise," I told him as we made ourselves comfortable on the soft cushions.

"My father writes," he confessed. "He's been writing fiction under a different name for about ten years now and his books are selling very well. But his biggest kicks are when he hears people talking about them in his shop. He'll have long discussions with his customers about them, really enjoying their comments and criticisms. He knows they're valid ones because the customers don't know he's the author."

I was fascinated. "How terrific!" I said. "That's really great!"

"Anyhow, Mariah, if you ever get anything written that you think he might like to check over, I'm sure I can get him to look at it and maybe give you a few pointers."

We sat in silence for a few minutes, breathing in the clean desert air, the sky a black velvet full of sequins of twinkling stars.

And finally, "I know they're just sitting there, waiting for me, Mariah," he said, standing up. "I'll be glad when that doctor hands me a clean bill of health so I can get on with living."

I stood up too and he encircled me in his arms. "I'll talk to them about the tram. I'll see what I can do."

My mouth met his in a sweet, velvet touch, like the softness of a butterfly I had once held in my hand a long time ago. But the butterfly's tenderness had been short-lived—I had watched it die right there in my hand.

A cloud slid in front of the moon and the night darkened as we parted.

Chapter 14

So it was with total surprise that my mother answered the phone just a few days later, to find Mrs. Strobe on the other end. My mother turned from the phone, holding her hand over the mouthpiece. "She says Paul can go up on the tram. She wants to know when it will be convenient for you to go."

I was just as surprised. "What's wrong with tomorrow?" I asked, quickly recovering. "Tomorrow, before she changes her mind."

My mother handed me the phone. "I'm free tomorrow." My voice cracked and trembled when I spoke.

"Fine," Mrs. Strobe said, but her voice sounded far away and cold. She quickly followed the one word with, "Goodbye," and then, "I just wanted you to hear it directly from me that it is all right with us."

I thanked her and hung up.

"Ahh," my mother said, smiling. "Mrs. Strobe is at last letting Paul crawl out of the family nest. I think she may let him fly off on his own now."

Paul's mother puzzled me. She seemed to love Paul so much, she was almost smothering him with it. My mother was so different. I knew every minute she loved me and Kim, but she never babied us.

I remember when Kim had first started to walk. She would wrap her finger tightly around my mother's, so fearful that my mother would let go. Mom didn't like that and eventually came up with a great idea. She held a clothespin in her own fingers and let Kim hold onto that while she walked. Finally when my mother was confident that Kim was strong enough, she let go of the clothespin. Kim, unknowing, went jauntily along by herself, still thinking she was holding onto my mother's finger. My mother had left her with something to hold onto until she had gained more confidence in herself. After a while Kim was sure of herself and she dropped the clothespin. She never had to crawl again.

"Kim will want to go, too," I told my mother. I'd always dragged my little sister everywhere but this time I wasn't about to give in easily.

My mother was sitting at the kitchen table where she'd been going over her books for her entrance exam. She looked up and smiled at me. "No, not this time," she said, and I thought I'd die with happiness. "While you were at the Strobes' that night, Judy's mother called and she and Judy will be driving down here on Sunday. The three of us will be going to the tram then."

She got up slowly and poured me a cup of coffee. Placing it down in front of me, she said, "No, I'm sorry, but you'll just have to go with Paul—alone."

I felt as if my mother had finally handed me the clothespin—and she herself had stepped back. She trusted me completely. I knew I could never disappoint her.

At eight o'clock the next morning, Paul knocked at the kitchen door. "I bear gifts," he said when I opened the door.

"What?" I asked.

"They're not for you. They're for Kim," he said, smiling.

Kim appeared out of nowhere. "I heard my name," she yelled.

"Don't yell. We can all hear you," I told her.

Paul thrust a package into her hands. "I was thinking. . . . I've watched you out in the backyard on the picnic table, coloring those books of yours. You seem to really enjoy it, but I think you should be drawing your own pictures instead of following someone else's lines."

My mother appeared in the kitchen then and I knew she had heard his comments.

"I've brought you some drawing paper and pencils. Then, here I have charcoal and a few other items. A set of brushes, some watercolors, and oh, yes, a book on art for the beginner."

From out of another large paper sack, he pulled several pieces of canvas, all different sizes. Each was mounted on pieces of wood and he told her that if she did a good job on each one, he would frame them all himself.

Kim sucked in her breath and then yelled, "Whew!" Her eyes grew wide with delight and suddenly she threw her arms around his neck and kissed him hard on the cheek. "Thank you,

Paul. Oh, thank you!" I swear there were tears in her eyes.

Paul had captured another Johnson, I thought, smiling to myself. I think you could safely say, we all three loved him now.

Paul and I left the house, dashing through the backyard, hurrying to be on our way to a great day.

"Well, my lovable wench," Paul said as he went out the back gate, "are you sure you wish to spend the day with such a serf forever, never knowing the richness I offer you as the Lord of the Strobes!" He was imitating the language in the novel I had lent him.

"Paul." I laughed and yelled at him. "Paul, you're crazy! But you read it, didn't you? What do you think?"

He flung open the door of his car for me. "Into the carriage, my plucky little creature, and you will know the scarlet passion that dwells within this hairy chest."

I was ready for him when he crawled in his side of the car. My bag with my comb and brush and lipstick and Kleenex was fairly heavy, and it bounced neatly off the side of his head.

"Hey, Mariah. You *are* plucky!" he screamed, trying to defend himself. With a roar of the motor we were off, laughing like little kids. Our beautiful day was about to begin.

"You've got your sweater?" Paul asked me after a while, after our kidding each other had subsided. "It's about forty degrees cooler up there." It seemed almost impossible. We would be in the little cable car only about fourteen minutes, he'd told me, and yet we would experience an enormous change in temperature.

We turned into Tramway Road and immediately the road started climbing. "We'll drive up to where we'll park and hop on an open bus," Paul explained. "This climbing is hard on cars—notice the barrels of water alongside the road. It's such a steep incline, a lot of cars overheat."

We were finally coming into a parking area swarming with cars. I was surprised to see so many people doing the same thing we were doing. "You should see it around Christmas holidays and Easter," Paul said as we settled ourselves on the open bus. "It gets so bad, you have to wait for your number to be called just to board the little cable cars."

The bus heaved and moaned as it climbed up the mountain. Finally we slid into another parking area. "We're already at two thousand, six hundred and forty-three feet," Paul told me, pointing out the sign. I nodded and was feeling the temperature change already.

We entered Valley Station and I followed Paul over to the ticket booth. People were everywhere, some of them lined up by the windows, watching for the cable car to descend.

"They go up every half hour," Paul told me. "One is always going up while the other is coming down. Come on, let's go outside and watch."

"How many people can go up at one time?" I asked.

"About eighty," Paul said, checking on the tickets in his hand. "You can even take up skis in the winter or camping equipment. Last winter Joe and I brought up our skis and the summer before, we came up twice and set up camp in the woods."

I looked up at the huge cables where soon the little car would appear. It scared me to death. "I don't know if I want to go," I told Paul lamely. "What if the thing breaks? What if the lines get tangled?"

Paul laughed. "I can tell you're going to be a good writer," he said. "Most writers are 'what-if' people, my dad says."

I poked him in the ribs with my bony elbow. "Come on, Paul, tell me you're not just a little bit scared when you go up in that thing, no matter how many times you've done it!"

Paul laughed again and then grabbed for my hand. "Look, it's coming down now. Let's walk over and see if we can squeeze in that line."

We must have been numbers seventy-nine and eighty because they closed the gate right after we entered. We were the last two to hop onto the canary-yellow car.

"Now at this very minute, there's a cable car just like this one at the top of the mountain, getting ready to come down," Paul said. I shivered. Even if Paul wouldn't admit it, I bet he was a little scared, too.

"Right smack in the middle of the ride, we'll meet the other car," Paul told me.

Suddenly the car lurched forward. There

was no time for me to change my mind. To my amazement, I seemed to be the only person on the little car who showed any fear at all. Everyone else was laughing and talking, some of them carrying camping gear, binoculars, and cameras. The calm, fun-filled atmosphere helped me start to relax a little.

"I wish I'd brought my camera," I told Paul.

Over the loudspeaker a male voice pointed out signs of interest along the way. "The tramway is a double-reversible operation with enclosed cable cars operating in opposite directions, each suspended from its own set of double-track cables. It is the largest double-reversible passenger carrying tramway in the world," the voice droned on. "It was opened to the public in September of 1936."

I looked up at Paul. "My ears are closing up," I told him. "Are yours?"

"Not yet," he said. "Try swallowing hard. Here." He pulled out a stick of peppermint gum. "Chew on this. It'll help."

"When you step out," the voice over the loudspeaker said, "you will be at our Mountain Station which is eight thousand, five hundred and sixteen feet above sea level."

At the halfway point the other little cable car coming down was suddenly right beside us. The people in the other car waved and Paul and I waved back, smiling. "Whew," I said. "And this goes on all the time, up and down this mountain! I wonder how many people—"

The voice suddenly boomed out, "Our cable

cars named Crocker and Coffman, after the two men who made it all possible, have carried over two million visitors to Tramwayland to share in a dream that is now a reality."

"Well, there's your answer," Paul said and we both broke out laughing.

My ears were getting worse so I chewed the gum harder. I could see huge evergreens now against the hard slabs of mountain. "How on earth did they get the material up here to build the towers that support this whole thing?" I whispered to Paul.

"Helicopters," he told me. "I saw the movie once when I was up here with Mom and Dad. They show it free at the Mountain Station."

The sides of the mountain were changing colors with more evergreens in sight. A small animal darted through the thick foliage.

"It's already beautiful," I said to Paul.

"Aren't you afraid anymore?" he laughed, pulling me close to him.

"Just a little," I admitted. "I guess I'm getting used to it."

We had reached the huge building called the Mountain Station. The cable car slid to a stop and the door opened to let the people pile out. Paul grabbed my hand and together we entered the station. Signs pointed the way to the Alpine Restaurant and the gift shop. One sign pointed to a lower level advertising a game room on the ground floor.

Crossing over a large open area, Paul ushered me through another door and suddenly we were outside again. "We'll follow one of the hiking trails," Paul said. "When you get tired, we'll go back and have something to eat."

We stood at the top of the winding trail, a path that wound downward into the forest below. The tall evergreens stood silent all around us, the trail carpeted with their needles. The only sounds were songs of birds, and a few happy voices of children sifting through the branches of the sweeping trees. Their branches swayed like deep velvet drapes.

"This is so beautiful, Paul," I said in a whisper for fear that even the sound of my voice would break the spell. "I don't need a camera," I told him. "I'll remember this day as long as I live."

"In the winter, it's entirely different," Paul said, taking my hand as we followed the trail. "It's like someone took all of this and topped it with whipped cream."

I was looking down, watching for vines and exposed roots on the trail so that I wouldn't stumble, when I saw it. It was a tiny bird, a pretty one with blue and white feathers. When I knelt down to inspect it closer, I realized it was dead. Paul bent down alongside me.

"The little thing is dead, but hasn't been for too long," he said. "It still has a little warmth left in its body."

"The poor thing," I said sadly. "And it looks so terribly young. I wonder why it died so young?"

"I guess it was its time to die," Paul said, standing up. "Mariah, let's bury it. I mean, it would be better than just leaving it here to be torn apart by some animal."

He walked around looking under the huge trees and then bent down and picked up a jagged rock and a stick. "We can dig a small grave with these."

Together we knelt and gouged out the bird's final resting place. When it seemed deep enough, I dug into the bottom of my handbag and pulled out my old scarf. I'd used it hundreds of times on the beach to tie back my hair. It was time I bought a new one anyway.

"We'll wrap him in this," I told Paul. "It seems proper that he should be wrapped in something."

I spread out the pale yellow scarf on the dark earth. Paul gently picked up the little dead thing and placed it on the scarf, wrapping it with care. Then he placed the bundle into the grave and together we brushed the earth back over the hole. Paul stood up and stamped the ground down firmly with his shoes. It was an odd but beautiful moment between us, one I always remember.

We walked further up the trail. "Have you ever lost someone, someone you really loved— through death, I mean?" Paul asked, finally throwing away the stick.

I thought for a moment. "No. No, I really haven't," I told him. "I had a great-aunt who died just a few months ago, but I can truthfully say, I didn't really even know her. I felt sorry, of course, but I can't really say I loved her. No, I've never lost anyone close to me through death. But I know someday I will have to."

Paul was silent as we walked on. The trail twisted and turned and with each turn was even more beautiful.

"I had a dog," Paul said finally. "He was a funny mixture, cocker spaniel and poodle, and he looked something like a dirty old throw rug. He'd wandered onto our property when I was about four. Mom let me keep him and he was the most loyal friend anyone could have.

"And then one day, when he was pretty old and half-blind, he ran after a car and somehow got caught under the back wheels. He died in my arms, his big brown eyes searching mine, asking me what happened."

"Oh, I'm sorry," I told Paul.

"Well, anyhow," Paul said, "the point of the story is, my grandfather lived with us. He was my father's father and a great old man. He used to bring me up here, even when he was in his eighties. We'd trudge around this place, and I'd forget he was so old.

"After my dog died, I was pretty miserable. I wouldn't eat or talk. I was being a real brat and my mother didn't know what to do for me. It was then that my grandfather brought me up here. We sat down under the evergreens near a little brook around here, and he talked to me.

"I wish you could have known my grandfather. He was tall and very strong. Toward the end he got very thin, but he was still a strong man for his age. He had a huge clump of white hair, and it fell over his eyes when we hiked along this trail."

Low evergreen branches blocked our trail and Paul held them aside for us to pass. Before long, the brook Paul had spoken of came into sight. For a long time I had heard the water splashing over the rocks, flowing down and over the pebbles, but I had no idea it was so close. Paul sat down on the forest floor and removed his shoes and then walked into the shallow stream.

"Come on in," he called to me. "It feels great!"

"Did your grandfather make you feel better by bringing you up here?" I asked, removing my own shoes. He was right. The cool water felt good on my dusty, hot toes.

Paul knelt down and picked up a shiny pebble. "Yes, but it wasn't just this place. It was what he told me. He said that people don't really die if we keep a good memory of them. He said, if we just think about the loved one once in a while, then that person always remains alive for us."

"What do you mean?" I asked, finally coming out of the stream and throwing myself on the cool ground under a tree.

"Well, I tried it," Paul said, following me out of the stream. "Every time I felt bad about my dog, I'd bring up old memories of him. Sometimes I'd even laugh out loud when I thought about all our good times together. It really worked. He seemed to come alive, to stay alive whenever I just thought of him."

I sat back against the tree and hugged my knees. "And your grandfather?"

"He died last year," Paul said. "But he prepared me well for it. You see, he never really died for me. I can keep him forever, if I just sit down once in a while and remember him. Inside of me he will live forever. Mariah, I bet you think I'm crazy."

"You're not crazy, Paul," I said. "Maybe you found the secret to the pain of death for the survivors. If it works for you, it could work for others."

Although he wouldn't admit it, I could tell the hike had tired out Paul. So I persuaded him to stay with me by the brook, resting and enjoying a beautiful day together.

I said to Paul so many times, "I had no idea this was all here. It's funny, when you come into Palm Springs, you look up at the mountains and they seem to be only cold slabs of granite. If you look really hard, you can see some of these trees, but from down there you just never can imagine that this is all up here."

"And so many people never even look up," Paul said with an edge to his voice. Then he was silent for a long time. I had the feeling that if he could, he would kidnap every person who even came near his beautiful town and force them to discover its inner secret wonders.

When he wasn't looking, I stared long and hard at him. His handsome features were only part of his beauty—the important part was the beautiful person he was inside. I turned quickly when I realized he had caught me gazing at him. I didn't want him to know I worshipped him. Wasn't it dangerous to let a guy know how terribly much you loved him? The men in the Gothics pursued a woman until they knew they had won the battle and then they dropped the poor girls like hotcakes. But that seemed too dramatic for real life. I was afraid Paul would get scared if my feelings were obvious.

On our way back to the tram, he grabbed my hand and pulled me over to a tree. "I don't want you to get too tired," he told me, concern in his eyes.

I sat down quietly beside him, his face close to mine. His lips caught mine off guard, but his mouth was no longer gentle. I pulled away, but he caught me again. This time I responded, my mouth as eager as his. His hand touched my throat, his other arm around my waist. He stroked my throat, holding up my chin to seal our kiss. It became too much. I struggled, stopped, and gave my lips to him completely. But confusion filled me. Where was the tenderness? Our kiss felt like flames of fire.

Suddenly he pulled away. It was him pulling away, not me. He laughed nervously, stood up, and brushed the pine needles from his pants. He took my hand and helped me up.

"Mariah, I can almost hear my mom calling me—and from way down there. How could she possibly do it?" He was grinning. Perhaps Paul sensed my confusion or maybe he was afraid of his feelings, too. I was both glad and a little disappointed by his ending our embrace so abruptly.

We were both smiling though. "I know," I told him as we entered the pathway again. "And I think I'd better hold onto that clothespin for a while longer." He didn't understand me, but it didn't matter.

I remembered the vows I had made to myself, the day I talked to my mother about the reason for my father's leaving us.

When I fall in love, it will be for always. Nothing will change that. No one will walk out. We will stay together forever, and when death finally separates us we will have the memories that we shared. He will be that kind of person. I will know him instantly when I finally meet him. And he will love me forever. . . .

Silently, our hands touching, we headed back for the station.

Chapter 15

We both ordered a hot roast beef sandwich and a glass of root beer.

"My father would love it up here." I told Paul. I remembered how he loved evergreens and the woods full of moss and running squirrels.

"You still miss him very much, don't you?" Paul said, finishing every crumb on his plate.

"Oh, yes. I just wish—I just wish something good would happen and that he—"

"You know what I think, Mariah," Paul said. "It won't be any good if it isn't your mother's own decision. You can't, Kim can't bring him back. It's got to be her own wish, not yours. You could sit here and wish for one hundred years, and if he came back because of you or Kim it wouldn't work out."

I knew Paul was right. I finished my sandwich in silence.

"Let's go out to the observation porch," Paul said. "Don't forget your sweater."

We stepped out the side door to one of the observation terraces. "At night it must be a romantic sight," I said wistfully, hoping to recapture the feelings and emotions we had shared before.

"We'll come up here again sometime at night," Paul told me. "The only way I could get away from my mom this time was to promise her I would stay just a few hours."

"Aren't you feeling well?" I asked. Paul looked so well it was hard to imagine him ill at all.

"We have an old-fashioned doctor," Paul told me, pulling his jacket closer around him. "They believe anything he tells them—they trust him completely. Now he says I have to have a certain amount of rest and they accept that, no matter how I feel about it. No matter how I feel. Boy, I'll be so glad to get away to school."

We headed inside again. This time Paul steered me into the gift shop on the lower level. "I want you to have a souvenir," he said, taking me by the hand.

The gift shop was brightly lit with thousands of souvenir items. I touched one and then another and Paul just smiled at my confusion. Finally he put his hand up on a top shelf and pulled out a strip, a bumper sticker with black bold letters against bright yellow.

"P. S. I Love You," it read.

"Palm Springs, I love you—it's a popular bumper sticker," he told me. "But I want you to hang it somewhere in your room when you get home so that you'll remember this place and our day here."

He paid the girl at the counter and then handed the bag to me. "Thanks, Paul," I told him, knowing exactly where I would put it.

"Let's go out and look down at the city one more time," he said.

We stepped out on the terrace and peered down. Far below us lay the desert with its pale brown sand and prickly cactus. I could almost see the heat below. A silver airplane shot through the sky.

"Paul, do you draw, too?" I asked him then. "That was nice of you to give Kim all that art stuff. I think something will come of it."

"I fool around a little with it," Paul told me. "But what I'm really into, really serious about is architecture. I suppose drawing would go hand in hand with that. My mother loves art, all kinds of artwork, and she kinda wished it on me by buying me all the material years ago. She's thrilled I'm into architecture now."

"Then you draw buildings and houses—"

"I'm going to *build* buildings. Big ones. I like drawing and sketching houses too, but I think my thing will be skyscrapers for offices. Maybe someday if I get to be very good, I might even attempt some kind of a cathedral."

He took one look at his watch and frowned. "But all that will have to wait," he said. "Right now we've got to head for all those ants down there."

Again we climbed into the tram, but this time I wasn't scared. The little cable car left the platform, sliding softly on the huge cables. A little dip, and we were gliding down toward the upward bound car. I sighed heavily. I really didn't want this day to end, but I didn't want Paul to battle with his mother either.

127

"She doesn't like me, does she?" I whispered to Paul, making sure the people around us couldn't hear.

"Who?" Paul asked. Then, not waiting for my answer, he continued. "Of course she does. It's just that she's worried about me. That old doctor has her a nervous wreck most of the time. He didn't have to ruin my whole summer like this. The operation could have waited for one of my school breaks. I'm convinced of it."

We were gliding into the Valley Station. I wasn't going to say it out loud. I was only planning on thinking it, but it just came out. "But, Paul . . . if you hadn't stayed on this summer, we might never have met."

He turned and smiled down at me, squeezing my hand as the tram came to a full stop. "That proves that sometimes good things come out of bad," he said.

"So you're going to be a writer," Paul said, as we got into the car to leave. "I did read parts of the book you gave me, but what kind of writing will *you* do?"

"Just like that," I told him.

We headed down the hill that would put us in Palm Springs again.

He turned to me looking serious. "Not like that."

"What?"

"I'd rather see you do something—something more real." He drove very slowly, as if he didn't want to hurry home.

"That's real," I told him, feeling annoyed that he hadn't agreed with my taste. "It's just

128

that the setting is centuries ago. It's supposed to be very romantic."

"But why don't you write about the things you know about? Then maybe after you get a little practice you can go on to those kind of stories—if you still want to, that is."

"Oh, Paul," I said and gave out with a sigh. "You sound just like Mrs. Peterson, my lit teacher. Coming from her, I can understand; she's so stuffy. But coming from you . . . well, I'm disappointed."

"What's wrong? Aren't the 1980s romantic enough for you?"

"Oh, never mind, you don't understand," I told him bitterly. "Anyhow, what are we arguing about? Maybe I won't be good enough to write about anything."

"Have you ever submitted anything?"

"Yes," I confessed. "About three or four poems to a couple of the magazines. I also sent in a short Gothic piece about a girl hiding in her rich uncle's old castle. I'd thought it was pretty good—until the rejection slip came."

"And what do you know about a girl hiding in her rich uncle's castle?" Paul asked, grinning wickedly.

I must have looked as hurt as I felt because Paul looked over once or twice until he realized why I was quiet.

"I'm sorry," Paul said tenderly, reaching over and touching my hand. "But I want you to do me a favor. When you get back home, start looking around at the people you live with, your friends and other people you meet. Study them and make a list of their traits, the things they might do in certain situations. Then start making little stories, incidents out of that."

I looked at him, still feeling a little hurt. Then my curiosity took over. "What do you know about this? Who told you that this is the way?"

"My dad," he answered.

"Oh." I couldn't argue with that, I thought.

After a few moments, I said, "Paul, it really scares me. I mean, I've read so many of the stories about getting published, and they say that even if you're very, very good, your chances of getting into print are so small. They say—"

"Do you believe you're good? That someday you will be good enough?" Paul asked. "I mean, do you really believe you are a writer?"

I took a deep breath. "Yes," I told him. "I really believe that someday I will be good enough to be published." I hadn't ever been so confident but somehow now I felt the certainty very deeply.

We were part of the ant colony in Palm Springs again.

"That's what it takes," he said. "There's a gift shop here in Palm Springs. The owner, a lady with absolutely no experience, filled it with rattan furniture and odd pieces from Hong Kong and India. Everyone thought she'd go under. At that time, rattan wasn't in style. Even my father thought she wouldn't make it. But the lady had faith in herself, and in her first few months of business she sold everything in stock. She told Dad later that she hadn't known she might go under. She had always loved rattan objects and didn't realize that for a while they were out of fashion. It's just like the bumblebee principle."

"What is that?" I asked, puzzled. "I've never heard of that."

"It has something to do with aerodynamics. An engineer can look at a bumblebee, analyze the wingspan and amount of lift obtained from the wing, calculate the body weight that has to be supported by the wing—and after making all the computations will come up with the conclusion that the bumblebee can't possibly fly. But the bumblebee doesn't know this and it flies anyway!"

I laughed. "That's amazing. So you think that the lady in the rattan shop succeeded because she had so much faith in herself. But how does that apply to me?"

"If you have faith in your writing, you will in all probability find your books in a book shop someday."

"But a lot of writers have faith in themselves and never see their dreams come true."

"Mariah, I'm not going to guarantee your stuff will be published if you just have faith in yourself. I'm just saying that *without* that faith there isn't a chance in the world."

We were approaching the Abbotts' back gate and before Paul switched off the ignition I stole another glance at him. At least from today on, I could write about a passionate kiss with all the authority I'd ever need.

Chapter 16

That night Jim came over to play backgammon with Kim. They sat in the kitchen, as my mother was making apple dumplings.

"Did you ever have a wife?" Kim asked out of the clear sky.

My mother gave her a dirty look that went right over her curly red hair. That's another funny thing about Kim. Dirty looks don't seem to bother her at all like they do me, but then there are a lot of years between six and sixteen.

"I did," Jim said, stirring his coffee. "I did indeed."

Kim was winning the round. "Let's double," she said to Jim. He agreed reluctantly.

My mother had finished plopping the dumplings into the baking pan and now was sliding them into the oven. "Don't you think you're getting a little personal, young lady?" she said to Kim, giving her another sharp look.

I'd been sitting at the opposite end of the table, doing my nails. I perked up my ears, listening to the rest of the conversation.

Jim raised his hand. "No, no. This here little girl's just merely interested in an old man's life," he protested. "Let the child be. I'll satisfy her curiosity."

Dropping the backgammon dice, the old man turned to Kim and began. "We lived out in the old backhouse, my Maryanne and me. I did the same things I'm doin' now and she was the maid. She was as pretty as a picture, my Maryanne, and much younger than me."

The apple dumplings began to fill the air with a delicious cinnamon and nutmeg smell. He went on.

"It was sad; the whole thing was so sad. Maryanne and me—we wanted children so bad, but nothin' ever happened. We talked some about adoptin' them, but we never went over to the agency to start the paperwork. Maryanne tried to drag me there a couple of times, but I just put it off. Then one day Maryanne left me. She went off with a man who used to help in the yard. She didn't even say goodbye. . . ."

"Oh," I said, feeling sorry for him. "But why didn't you go after her, fight for her?"

Jim laughed. "That's what I should have done," he said. "He left her a short while later and then Maryanne went to live with her sister in Kentucky. She was too ashamed to come back. Her sister wrote to me and begged me to come to Kentucky and get her."

"Why didn't you?" Kim asked, sneaking a peek in the glass oven door. My mother had stopped scrubbing the counter and had pulled over a chair and sat down.

"I couldn't," Jim said, shaking his head. "I

couldn't because I had this thin' in me I called *pride*. Oh, it was there all right. I was a very proud man. Then one day I went to one of my old buddy's funeral. I'd thought he was really old so I was surprised when I looked at the funeral announcement and found out that he was only one year older than me. That got me to thinkin'. I decided to go after Maryanne."

"And did you? Did she come back here?" Kim asked.

We all stopped breathing, waiting for his answer. It was so quiet; the only sound in the kitchen was the clock over the stove. I knew in my mind what Maryanne must have looked like. She had long black hair and she'd braided it and made a pretty bun high on top of her head. She'd had a beautiful face and figure. She had really loved Jim, but she somehow had been a little confused in what she really wanted —maybe the fact that she couldn't have children caused her to make the wrong decision. I looked up at Jim and waited for his answer.

"I got a vacation from the Abbotts and headed for Kentucky," he said, his eyes clouding over. "I went on the Greyhound bus. I hadn't told anyone so no one was waitin' for me at the terminal.

"Then I hitched a ride out to Maryanne's sister's place. God, what a forsaken, run-down place it was! I knocked at the door and there was Maryanne's sister, Sally, standing there, just a-lookin' at me like I was the devil himself. All of a sudden, she was beatin' on me, her little

134

skinny fists all over my head! And she was screamin' at the same time. 'Why now?' she was screamin' at the top of her lungs. 'Why now?'

"I grabbed her fists and untangled her arms and sat her right down on the old boards of the porch. She started to cry and I could hardly make her out. It was a little while before I could understand that my Maryanne had died just three days before. I'd arrived on the afternoon of her funeral. She'd gotten pneumonia. Sally told me that she didn't seem to want to live."

Jim bowed his head. "It's a shame," he said softly. "Time is so awfully short for us humans. We have no right to play God with it. If I had just stood still and listened to God, I'd have gone after her as soon as Sally had told me that she wanted me back. Seems a shame—and a terrible waste."

Jim got up; his eyes a bit clouded. He was still thinking about Maryanne. "Have to go back now," he said. "Tomorrow I have to cut the grass and maybe put in a few new bricks where they're breakin' up on the back paths."

He closed the screen door behind him and my mother got up to check the oven. "You girls finish watching the dumplings. They come out about eight-thirty. Mariah, cool them on the bread board, and be careful you don't burn your mouth—they'll be hot."

"Aren't you going to wait around for them?" I asked her.

"No," she said. "I've got a lot of mail to

answer. I'll eat mine in the morning." And with that she gave us each a peck on the cheek and disappeared down the hall.

Kim and I played three more games and then ate our dumplings in silence. Kim came out with it first.

"I wish Mom would go and get Daddy back—before it's too late," she said wistfully, biting into the hot dumpling and then taking a sip of her cold milk.

"I do, too," I told my little sister. "But, Kim, it's got to be her decision," I said, remembering my conversation with Paul. Why, I wondered, does love get so complicated sometimes? Would it be that way for me, too?

I cleared the table and went up to bed thinking about Jim and Mom and Dad and Paul.

Chapter 17

The morning after our tram trip, Paul called.

"I have the flu," he said, grumbling. "Or at least that's what we think it is. Mom said it should last just a couple of days. Dad had it two weeks ago, so I guess it's just going around. The only thing I can do is just stay in bed and drink a ton of juice."

I said all the things you're supposed to say to someone with the flu, but I'm sure my disappointment showed in my voice.

"I hope you don't get it, too," he said protectively. "Mariah, I'll come over as soon as this bug leaves me." His voice changed into a whisper then. "I love you, Mariah." My heart did another somersault.

He was waiting for me to say it back. How could this be? We'd known each other for such a terribly short time and yet somehow we both knew, *really* knew. "I love you, Paul," I said and I felt a catch in my throat.

For a moment I thought we'd been disconnected. "Don't move from that spot," Paul said at last in a commanding tone. "Don't do anything to hurt yourself, don't get sick, don't leave town. Just wait for me to get better, Mariah."

I laughed nervously. "Okay, Paul," I promised. "I'll wait for you to get better." His tone was disconcerting to me.

We said our goodbyes. My depression deepened as I went through the day helping my mother with some baking, drilling her with exam questions from one of her books. The summer was flying by and now Paul would be sick for another few days. It wasn't fair.

"The world hasn't come to an end," my mother said, stacking the clean dishes in the cupboard.

"Just about," I told her, brushing the crumbs off the kitchen tablecloth. "Just about."

The mail from Elaine was coming in each week and I answered each one faithfully. She wrote that she was having a great summer, and that she had met a boy on the beach. Lucky, I thought. I'd lived there my whole life and I'd never managed to meet one.

I started a journal which kept me busy, Kim and I fooled around in the pool for hours on end, and there was backgammon with Kim and Jim. But an entire week passed and still Paul was sick, so sick he couldn't even get out of bed. At least he could phone.

He called me every morning and every evening. We talked for about an hour until my mother started giving me dirty looks. Each time we spoke, his voice seemed to be getting weaker. I was getting more depressed every day. I had a feeling it was more than the flu that was keeping Paul in bed but he insisted I was wrong. He refused to have me worry about him.

"It's bad enough I've got a worry wart for a mother. I don't want my girl turning into a nervous wreck on my account."

Several times I drove down to Welwood Murray Library, and spent a couple of hours just sitting and thinking. It was just a little library, nothing like the one I often visit in Huntington Beach, but it made me feel right at home the minute I walked through the door. I wondered again if I'd ever have a book of my own in that library.

I walked over to the J's, where the books were arranged by the names of the authors. I found where Johnson would go, and when no one was looking, I pushed the other books aside slightly, making a space for my book. I stepped back and looked again and I could almost see it there. Feeling somewhat better, I finally pulled myself together and headed home.

Chapter 18

Paul had finally been allowed to get out of bed, but the first thing the Strobes did was to drag him off to the hospital for some more tests. This time they took him to a hospital in Los Angeles.

I watched them leave from the upstairs windows early that August morning. Later on in the day, when I went up to get my journal, I saw them return. They had been gone eleven hours.

Paul called me that night. "I really don't feel up to it tonight," he said, and his voice sounded far away. "But I'll beat you in backgammon tomorrow night, okay? You'd never believe all the junk they did to me today!"

We talked a little while and then he said goodnight. I put the backgammon set away and got out *TV Guide*.

"Damn!" I said out loud to the television set. My mother came into the room.

"Please, Mariah," she said, "you must have a bigger vocabulary than that."

"It's just that I'm feeling sorry for Paul," I told her. "I'm sure there's really nothing wrong with him, but his mother keeps telling him

140

that he's sick. Pretty soon he might begin to believe that."

"Nonsense," she said. "He's too bright a boy for that. And anyhow, Mariah. . . ." She came over close to me and sat on the footstool by my chair. "Anyhow, I think Paul is sick, *very* sick."

I looked down at her, startled. "Why, what makes you—"

"He's losing weight rapidly," she said, picking up her knitting. She'd been working on a baby sweater for one of the pregnant teachers at the school.

"He's just looking bad," she said. "I think maybe he's anemic; you know, maybe he's lacking in iron."

"But maybe it's the same thing Pete Baker had," I suggested, trying desperately to find an answer. "Remember they said he was just growing too fast. It's something that a lot of guys get when they are growing too fast."

"Maybe," she said, pulling the instruction booklet out of her bag. "Anyway, I'd suggest you postpone any hiking trips or things that could cause Paul to have a relapse. If he suggests anything strenuous, you say you'd just rather stay home and play backgammon or cards or something."

"I will," I promised. "But the summer is flying by and—"

"I know," my mother said, smiling now. "And I'm truly glad that you aren't still angry with me for dragging you here."

I'd completely forgotten that I'd been so

upset. It was hard to believe it now. I went up to my room that night and looked out at the darkness and then down at the gazebo. Paul just had to get well soon. I sat down with my journal and I wrote just one line that night. *"Please, God, let Paul get well—soon...."*

Chapter 19

About ten-thirty the next morning my mother knocked on my bedroom door. I'd overslept. She was planning on taking another shopping trip into town and I was supposed to be ready to go with her.

"Okay," I shouted. "I'm up!" At the same time I was jumping out of bed, she was pushing the door open.

"Mariah." There was a look of fear in her eyes. "Mariah, get dressed and come right downstairs! The Strobes are here!"

The Strobes? What could they want?

My mother went over to the closet and grabbed one of my tops and jeans. "Here, put these on," she commanded. "Hurry!"

"What's up?" I asked, running my fingers through my tangled hair.

"Just hurry," she commanded again and then she was out of the room, heading for the stairs.

She'd chosen a pretty top with sailboats on it and I wondered if I looked good enough for the Strobes as I quickly ran a brush through my hair. Were they here to scold me in front of my mother because Paul and I had tramped around so long that day when we went up on the tram? Were they blaming that trip for his bout with the flu?

I looked in the mirror. My eyes still looked sleepy. I wet my finger with my tongue and tried to smooth out my eyebrows. Oh, well, I'd have to go down and face whatever it was.

I could hear Kim down in the living room talking to Mrs. Strobe. She was asking how Paul was. "We all miss him so much," she was saying.

When I entered the living room all the talk stopped. Mr. Strobe quickly came over to me. "Mariah, Paul's gone. We can't locate him. He took his moped—it's gone from the garage."

"You mean he stayed out somewhere all night?" I backed up and sat down in one of the chairs. My fingers dug down deeply into the blue velvet arms. "Why would Paul do that?"

And then I looked over at Mrs. Strobe. She looked like she'd been crying for hours. "Oh, Martin," she said, sobbing. "Please tell them. Maybe they will be able to help." Mom asked Kim to run an errand and finally we were alone.

She was crying very hard then and even Mr. Strobe's consoling of her didn't help. "Please, Betty, please," he whispered gently, putting his arm around her.

I turned to my mother. She had gone a chalk-white. I turned from her to Mrs. Strobe who was trying to stop herself.

Mr. Strobe walked over to where I sat. "Paul is very upset, Mariah. You see, he must have gone into my study—maybe to get a book to read before he went to sleep. Anyhow, I had the papers on my desk—the ones from Dr. Ritter." That was Paul's Palm Springs doctor.

He wiped his eyes with his handkerchief and then he continued. "You see, Mariah, the papers were the doctor's forecast of Paul's condition."

"Condition?" I said, trying to find my voice. "What condition?"

Mr. Strobe coughed and then cleared his throat. "Paul's last tumor was malignant, Mariah. During the operation they found that the cancer had spread through his body. It was bad, so bad, they terminated any future plans to operate. They did what they could."

"And Paul was never told?" I said, feeling sick to my stomach.

"We thought in time...we were trying to find a way," Mr. Strobe said. "We both told the doctor that we wanted to do it our way."

Mrs. Strobe was crying again and this time my mother went over to her and sat next to her, gently touching her arm.

"And this paper you think he saw," I said in a whisper, "it said it just like that—in plain language—that there was something they wouldn't be able to fix?" The significance of those words was only now beginning to hit me. How could this be happening?

Mr. Strobe merely nodded his head.

"But the doctor is old—Paul told me," I said hysterically. "He's old. Maybe he doesn't know everything, the new things. Why, Paul told me—"

Mr. Strobe knelt in front of me, his eyes misting over, his hands shaking, reaching out

145

for mine. "The hospital in Los Angeles confirmed it. No, by no means, Mariah, will we stop here. There are great doctors all over the country—great hospitals we must look into. But right now . . . do you know where Paul could possibly be? Do you have any ideas at all? We've searched everywhere. We didn't call the police yet, but now—"

Frantically I looked up at my mother and then straight back at Mr. Strobe who was still kneeling in front of me. I could see it as clear as day. I could see Paul with his head bowed into his hands. I could see his tears falling from his eyes. He was sitting on a rock—his rock.

"I'll take you there," I told Paul's father.

Together we ran through the back gardens and then we crossed over the hidden path into the Strobes' garage. We didn't say another word as he helped me into his car. I showed him where to drive. How different this morning was from the happy one with Joe and Kim and Paul. Yet it was a beautiful sunny morning and this was the very same road.

I could almost hear the echoes of our laughter, like ghosts laughing. How strange that a morning could look the same, but that the people could be so different inside of themselves.

I showed Mr. Strobe where to stop. I wasn't sure if I could remember the exact spot. I'd been there only once. But I had to! I had to! I forced my brain to remember!

"I'll have to hike through the brush," I told him. "I know the way."

"I'll be right behind you," he said firmly, getting out of the car.

"No," I told him, just as firmly. "You can't come with me. Just sit here and wait in the car. I'll be okay. I don't know why, but I've got to go alone." An inner force I was never aware of before was propelling me forward, guiding my every action.

Mr. Strobe squeezed my hand. "Mariah, please find my son, please."

Chapter 20

The birds had heard the rumble of the car and had stopped their singing. They would begin again as soon as there was silence. I held my breath and hoped that I could remember where the rock was. I closed my eyes and squeezed them tightly. I wished desperately for the scene to fill the blackness behind my shaking lids. When I forced them open, I knew my wish had been granted.

Pushing back the thick branches of the trees and the high weeds, I finally came upon the little brook. I crossed over it and in just a few minutes I was in an area where the sun could break through. It shone down on the ground in lacy patterns, just like I'd remembered. When I looked around to the right I saw it shine down on the rock, Paul's rock, and there at the top of the slab, I saw a boy with his head bowed in his hands. Paul.

"Paul!" I cried out and my voice echoed somewhere far back in the canyon. A wild, startled look crossed Paul's face as he raised his head and saw me.

"Mariah." He struggled to a standing position. "Mariah! What are you doing here? Get out! For God's sake, go away!"

"Paul!" I cried out again, running toward the rock. "Your parents, they're worried sick!"

"Get back!" Paul yelled at me. "Don't come any closer!" He stooped to pick up something, a rock that he grasped in his right hand. "Don't come near me or I'll—I'll throw this at you! So help me, I will!"

Immediately I stopped in my tracks. "No, Paul. No, you can't mean it. You wouldn't do it." I tried to speak as calmly as possible.

"Just turn around and go back." He was pleading now, his arm slowly lowering the stone. "I warn you, go back! Don't come near me!"

I stood perfectly still, but my insides were shaking in fear. Fear, not for myself, but for Paul. And then I knew I had to move closer. Boldly I started toward the rock, and Paul raised the stone again. Deliberately I placed my feet in the little ledge that would lead me to the top of his rock. I saw him standing there above me, his hand still raised, his face stained with dirt and tears.

A few agonizing seconds later his hand slowly lowered and the stone fell harmlessly to the ground. He leaned over and with that same hand, he reached out and pulled me up to where he stood. Shuddering as if an icy wind had ripped through his body, he spoke my name again, "Mariah," but this time, softly, as he folded me into his arms.

"Mariah, Mariah." he breathed into my hair. "I just can't bear to have you see me cry...."

"It's okay," I whispered back. "I know they

say that a boy shouldn't cry, but I think it's okay if a man does."

The tears came freely then for both of us as we sat on Paul's rock. He told me how he'd felt when he had found the doctor's report. In blind anger he'd run to the garage and jumped on his moped. He'd torn through the night and finally had found himself at the reservation.

Hiding his moped in the brush, he had trudged through the weeds toward his rock. Throughout the night he'd called out to God, swearing bitter things at Him, trying to reason with Him, asking why his life had to be cut short. Why Paul Strobe?

"You see, I have so many things I have to do," he told me, the tears drying on his face. "I have to build buildings. I want to have my name on them. I want to teach someday. And then, even more important—I've been learning each day—even more important, there's you. . . ."

His fingers slowly untangled my hair. "Paul, your father said there are other doctors, good doctors who can do more, good hospitals. He said there's still so much hope. And I read some things about cancer. They're coming up with new treatments all the time."

"I'm not going to give up," Paul said, leaning against me. "When I first came here last night, I felt awful. I wanted to bash my head up against this rock and get it all over with. But as the night went on, I realized how dumb that was, how stupid I was acting. It would only have hurt my parents—and I could never hurt them. I was just pulling myself together, but then you came—and the panic in me started all over again."

When he said parents, I remembered Mr. Strobe. "Oh, Paul, your father's waiting in the car; your parents are frantic. We have to let them know you're okay."

"In a few minutes," he said.

Although we said nothing then, the silence between us was as full of meaning and feeling as if we were holding a long conversation, a talk of our love, our devotion to each other. In the silence I could feel we were exchanging vows to be in love forever.

Finally I had to break the magic spell. "Paul, your father..."

Together we slid down the rock. Paul stopped by the little brook and knelt beside it. It was almost dry in the summer months, but there was enough water trickling through it to wash his face. He combed back his hair with his fingers and then took my hand.

"I'm ready," he said.

Together we left our magic wilderness for the last time.

Chapter 21

It's hard to tell when summer is over in Palm Springs. The signs are subtle—the absence of the high school and college kids for instance. The big families, too, are gone from the motels and the owners heave a sigh of relief.

The shops that have been closed for the summer are opened, dusted out, and the new signs go in the window, Open. See Our New Fall and Winter Line of Fashions, or Come In and Browse—Please No Bare Feet or Food.

The really very rich people come in the month of November, right after Thanksgiving, Paul told me. We were leaving.

I said goodbye to Paul in his hospital room where he was undergoing a brand new treatment. Soon he would be moved to a hospital in Houston, Texas, where he would undergo more tests and more treatments. He said he felt like a guinea pig, but that someone had to do it so that someday we could lick cancer completely. He had lost so much weight and his color scared me.

"I'll find some way to visit you in the new hospital, Paul," I promised that last day in

Palm Springs. "Mom said she'll get the money together so I can take the bus. It's the cheapest way."

Paul bent over and kissed the tips of my fingers. "One thing I want you to do. I want you to write me a story, okay? And send it to me as soon as you've finished. I want to be your critic!"

I smiled at him. "Okay," I promised.

Kim was saying her goodbyes. "Next time I'll beat you at backgammon," she told him.

"Next time we play for real money." Paul laughed and his laugh sounded so hollow to me. I looked up at my mother and she avoided my eyes. She had been standing off to one side, looking out the hospital window, keeping a safe distance. She knew Paul and I wanted to say a private goodbye.

"When Mariah sends me her manuscript, you can send me one of your drawings," Paul said to Kim.

"I will," Kim said, but her voice shook.

Mr. and Mrs. Strobe came in then and since visitors were limited in Paul's room, we had to leave. They shook our hands and told us to have a safe trip home. We already had our bags and things packed in the car. We'd said goodbye to Old Jim who was watching the house until the Abbotts arrived in another day or so.

Paul took one look at his parents and then grabbed his mother and whispered something in her ear. She turned to me and said, "Mariah, wait a minute. Paul wants to talk with you."

I watched as everyone left the room and

then I went over to Paul's bed. He looked shorter, all laid out like that, and his legs looked like skinny poles under the sheets.

He put out his long thin arms and encircled me into them. Gingerly I lowered myself to his chest and held him tight. We kissed and then I pulled away, turning my head toward the window. I had not intended to let him see me cry, but the tears jumped right out of my eyes and spilled down.

He held me straight out from him and said, "Mariah, we've both cried enough for now. From now on we'll spend the rest of our time laughing and living every minute we have left." He was my old Paul again.

"You understand about my mother," he said, wiping away my tears with the sheet. "She never hated you and over the past few weeks she's learned to love you as my father has. She wanted so badly to see me get well, so much that she thought rest could do it. She always thought in the back of her mind that if only I had enough rest, the doctors could be proved wrong."

"I know," I told him. "My mother told me that she felt your mother was doing what every good mother would do."

"Okay," Paul said. "I wanted to get that straight. Now there's a good possibility that if things go right with the new treatments, there's a chance I might be coming back home sooner than you thought."

I forced a smile. "Yes, Paul." In my heart I

154

knew only a miracle would bring him back home, but I was glad he hadn't given up hope.

"I'll write to you," he promised. "I'll let you know how things are going. I want you to visit me, of course, but please don't come without telling me. I mean, I want to have my hair combed at least—and I don't want you to catch me with a pretty nurse!"

"About the letters you will write me," I told him, "If it gets to be too much of an effort, the hospitals have nurses' aides who can write them for you."

"What do you think, I'm an invalid or something?" he said, and we both laughed so hard that the Strobes looked in through the half-open door to see what was going on.

I bent and kissed him once more. "So long, Paul," I whispered.

"So long," he whispered back. I backed away slowly, not wanting to leave. He held onto my arm and then his hands slid down to my hand and he held my fingers and then just the tips of them and then finally we weren't touching anymore.

"Eat your chicken soup," I said, blowing him a kiss from the hallway.

Kim and my mother and the Strobes were waiting in the hall. "I've said my goodbye," I announced to them. I don't even remember walking out of the hospital and getting into the car.

Chapter 22

The long road leading out of Palm Springs stretched in front of us. It had been only ten weeks since I had been on the road, yet I felt a lifetime older.

The car hummed along and neither Kim or my mother or I felt like talking. The wind was still, unusual for this road, I thought.

"I guess we can safely wind all the windows down," my mother told us.

Kim was sketching a picture of the Abbott house. I turned around and looked at it. "That's great!" I told her. "Paul wants to be an architect, you know."

There was a heavy silence in the car. I looked over at my mother who was giving her full attention to the road and then I looked over at the blue mountains and again saw the tiny sticks that were really great pine trees. Would I ever go up there again—and would it be with Paul?

My mother finally spoke. "There is a lot of hope for curing Paul, you know," she said. Was she saying it for me or was she just trying to convince herself?

"I know," I said, just for something to fill the void. "I know." But inside I was thinking.

"With all their money, why can't they save their son?"

"It is one of the finest hospitals in this country," my mother said, still keeping her eyes on the road.

I felt suddenly very angry. "With everything they've invented and discovered. . . . Why—why can't they do something about this!" My sudden burst of anger even surprised me.

My mother shook her head. "I don't have an answer for you, Mariah," she said. "I guess money can't buy everything after all." My mother had spoken my own thoughts out loud.

Suddenly the wind came up as we rounded a bend in the road. It howled fiercely, shaking our car with unexpected fury. The wind is angry, too, I thought as I quickly rolled up my window, but not nearly as angry and frightened as I was.

We entered the freeway and the winds died down. Again we fell silent, my mother just concentrating on the road ahead of her; Kim dedicated to her drawings. At least she had advanced from her crayons and coloring books, I thought. In a little while she fell asleep and I turned to watching fields of dry weeds fly by us. If it didn't rain within the next few weeks, a fire would start for sure. The flames would creep up the mountain sides while we watched helplessly on television. It was the same year after year ever since I could remember.

But it hadn't meant much to me before. I had never realized that there were beautiful, stately green trees on the tops of those mountains, a land of peace and beauty, and they could be wiped out in only one day.

"Mariah, I was going to wait until we arrived home," my mother started to say, interrupting my thoughts, "but in the quiet of the car we will be able to discuss it even better."

I looked over at my mother, her hair tied back by a dark blue scarf; her eyes were still glued to the road. Suddenly I felt like something big was going to happen, something very important.

"I've been writing to your father," she said slowly. "I haven't made any decisions yet, but I'm thinking about asking him to come back. How would you feel about that?"

I took a deep breath and blinked. Turning to my mother, I looked at her again. Behind her dark glasses, I saw a very tiny teardrop edging out over the side of her eye. I could see it because I was sitting right beside her and she could not just walk away from me as she had done so many times before when we had discussed my father.

"I'm waiting for you to answer, Mariah," she said without taking her eyes from the road.

I took another deep breath. "Having Dad back is one of the most important things in my life," I told her evenly.

I could see her mouth relax. "That night Old Jim spoke about his wife ... it made me think about the old saying—forgive and forget. Your father hurt me, Mariah, hurt me in a way that I think you're only now beginning to understand. I don't know if I can do it, but I think I'm willing to try to forgive him." The tears were flowing freely now.

Very carefully she slowly cut the speed of the car and drove off the freeway onto a shoulder. Then she pulled a tissue from her bag. Lifting her sunglasses away from her eyes, she dabbed at the tears that were by this time spilling all over the place. "His leg is so much better now," she went on. "He's coming back to Laguna Beach. He's even arranged for the insurance company to take him back, the same one he worked for before, before—"

"Oh, Mom, that's great," I said. For the moment I forgot about Paul and grew excited about seeing my father again.

"I don't want to get your hopes up—not yet—and I don't want you saying anything to Kim. I'm going to take it very slowly. I want to be sure I'm making the right decision."

"Whatever you decide, Mom, I'll be with you," I said, patting her arm.

I looked over at her. I knew that it would be difficult for her to forget the past; in time I was convinced it would all heal over. Then she could take Dad back. I also knew a few scars were bound to remain. I wished so hard at that moment that I could help her, but I could hear Paul telling me to just be still. I could remember what he said to me that day—her own decision. It would all come out right. I just knew it.

Carefully she entered the slow lane and then gradually speeded up and entered the middle lane, where she liked best to drive.

Chapter 23

Kim and I had the car doors open even before my mother had turned off the motor. "Take your share of stuff into the house," my mother yelled at us.

The Gretels had left the night before and so the red roses in the gold vase on the dining room table were still fresh. My mother slid the little card out of its envelope. "Thank you for a wonderful summer. We fell in love with your house. The Gretels."

She put her face down into the flowers and breathed in the sweet smell. "How nice," she said. "What a nice thing to do."

I ran upstairs, heading for my bedroom. Propped up on my chest of drawers was a folded note. I grabbed it and sat down on my bed. It felt good to be home in my old familiar room, but somehow the house seemed so much smaller to me. Of course, it was just that the Abbott house had been so huge.

Dear Mariah,

I will miss your home, your room and your wonderful ocean. Mostly, though, I will miss your rock where I have spent many hours alone, enjoying the sounds of the waves. Although I am anxious to start the new school year, I wish my summer could have been longer, because of your beautiful, sunny house and your lovely letters. I wish you much success.

Your friend,
Elaine Gretel

I fell asleep that night thinking of Paul. I wondered what he was doing, wishing I could be with him. Later that evening my mother came up to check on me and found me sound asleep, holding Elaine's letter in my hand.

Chapter 24

The morning sun woke me, streams of it flowing through my bedroom window like gold ribbons, the yellow and white curtains trying to loosen themselves from the rods blown by the brisk ocean breeze.

I was anxious to be off, to head for my rock and run along the edges of the water, sticking my toes into the cool incoming streams. It would feel so good again to squiggle my feet into the damp sand.

Later in the day, was I surprised when I saw Amy. She had lost at least ten pounds!

"Mariah, Mariah!" she called to me. "I'm so glad you're home!" She looked so different, I still couldn't believe it. She actually had her hair curled!

"Dad took me to a health spa and a fancy New York beauty shop for my birthday and I got a perm," she said when we finally ran into each other in the middle of Talbot's meadow.

We threw ourselves down into the tall weeds and just looked at each other. "I really can't believe it," I told her. "You look so great, so much thinner—and your hair looks terrific!"

She smiled. "Yes, and Mom's having me fitted for contact lenses next week," she told me. "Just think, Mariah, I'm going to be able to throw away those glasses!" Her pleasure was contagious and we sat there beaming at each other. "But why didn't you write, you stinker, not even a postcard! And I sent you six!"

I knew that was coming. "I'm sorry," I told her and explained about not remembering to get her New York address. "And we were terribly busy besides," I added. "We had to keep the house nice and do shopping, and I spent a lot of time at the library—and then there was Paul." I almost wanted to keep Paul a secret, a private thing that was all mine but my eagerness to show Amy how I'd grown up won.

She sat up straight and pushed some weeds away from her hair. How would I ever tell Amy that I'd learned that boys weren't all so bad—in fact some were definitely terrific.

"Who's Paul?" she demanded.

"Just some guy I met," I told her casually. "He's very nice and he took us a lot of places that I would have never found on my own."

"Oh," Amy said, chewing on a piece of grass. "Do you think you'll ever see him again?"

"Oh, yes," I said, sounding *so* sophisticated. "We're very good friends, and we—"

"You mean he's your boyfriend?" Amy's eyes were round and getting bigger. I couldn't tell if she was hurt or pleased—or just shocked. I didn't know how or what to say, not sure she'd understand.

"Well, yes, except that right now Paul is

163

sick. He's going to have to be in the hospital for a little while."

"Oh." She sank back in disappointment. "Oh, well, when he gets better, you can always go see him. Palm Springs isn't that far."

"I know." I would save the bad news for another day. No reason to say anything yet. No reason to tell her that it might take a long, long time for Paul to get better, or maybe even worse, that maybe Paul could never get better. I tried to smile, but it didn't feel very sincere. At least Amy let the subject drop for which I was grateful.

We got up out of the tall blades of grass and headed for Amy's house. "I want you to see my bedroom," Amy said. "Mom got back from Iowa sooner than she thought she would, so she thought she'd surprise me and give me a whole new room. She stashed away all that kid stuff—at last—and then she did everything in blues and greens. It's fantastic."

I followed right behind her up the stairs. "Maybe we could go to the movies down in Laguna tonight," I suggested. "I'm sure I can get the car." I wanted to keep busy, I realized, so I wouldn't think about Paul.

But just as she got to her bedroom door, Amy turned. "Oh, I'm sorry, Mariah, but I have a date tonight. Last week, when I got back from New York, I met a guy. His name is Kirk Bentley. I'm going to the movies with him tonight." Well, perhaps Amy would understand about Paul and me after all, I thought.

I smiled as I followed her into her shiny,

new bedroom. The room looked more like a den than a bedroom, a decided improvement over the juvenile junk that used to litter her room. It had been quite a summer for both of us. Funny how many things can change in only two months of summer when you've finally turned sixteen. . . .

Chapter 25

The fall rolled by quickly, each day's routine meshing into the next. Mom and Dad were seeing each other occasionally, but Mom was determined to take things one day at a time and refused to make a final decision yet.

In any case, it was great having him back in Laguna again. He had a small apartment near his office and sometimes Kim and I would spend the night with him. At first it was a little awkward trying to make up the two years he'd been gone, but both of us tried very hard to learn all we could about each other. One night I even told him about Paul and he truly seemed to understand the mixture of heartache and joy I was experiencing.

The days before Thanksgiving were filled with housecleaning, helping my mother getting ready for the holidays. Already Christmas stuff was appearing in the stores down in Laguna Beach.

I went with my mother to buy our turkey and we lugged home yams and day-old bread for stuffing and cabbage for the cole slaw and goodies to bake the pumpkin and mince pies.

The air was crisp and sweet, a little cool for this time of year.

I looked up at the mountains. They were topped with snow and looked like cupcakes topped with frosting. The ocean was still mildly warm, but I hated to see it get so dark so early.

Eleventh grade had not been as hard as I had thought it would be, and Amy and I seemed to be getting through it pretty easily. She was dating Kirk Bentley exclusively and seemed to be very happy. I spent most of my spare time just writing to Paul in Texas. Once a week he wrote back.

His life was busy with treatments and tests. "Experiments," he called them, and he even went to classes, too. "We wheel ourselves into a large room and we have different instructors who come and go," Paul told me. "My parents have brought me loads of books and I am learning a lot more than I probably would have if I had attended my regular classes at college, or at least that's what they tell me here. I feel I am getting better now. I should be, with all they're doing to me. But I miss you, Mariah. If you could be here with me, I wouldn't mind all of this too much, but I would rather have you wait and see me all well when I return to Palm Springs.

"I'm told that it should be sometime after Christmas, perhaps in January, the early part. At least that's what I overhear when the doctors talk together. I'm a great eavesdropper, Mariah, because I like to know what's going on. After all, it is my body they're talking about.

"Do you remember the day I first showed you the reservation? I think I loved you—even then."

I wrote in my journal faithfully as Paul had asked me to. Elaine and I exchanged letters almost every week. I told her about being named assistant editor of the school paper. I was very proud of that. I put away the romance novels, stacking them carefully in boxes and then carrying them out to the garage. With the school-work and my journal, all my letter writing and the school paper, I would just have to wait a little while longer until I had more time to write a whole book. Anyhow, I had promised Paul I would write a story about me first, and every-day things like they are today.

Chapter 26

November 22, Thanksgiving

Dear Mariah,

As you will no doubt notice, this is not my handwriting. Pearl, the volunteer for this section, is helping me by writing because my right hand is a little weak from the needles they put in it yesterday. But the reason I am writing is that I want to tell you that I feel I am getting better. Yes, better!

You mentioned in your last letter to me that your mother will give you enough money to fly to Texas during the holidays. Please don't. I mean, I want to see you, but I want to see you when I am completely well. You must understand. Would you want me to see you if you were a little under the weather? Try, Mariah, try to understand how I feel about this. I want to look great when I see you again!

I woke up last night and had this sudden surge of strength. I haven't felt so good in a long time—since I came here. I talked to Dr. Shue this morning and he just smiled. Maybe he has

169

some kind of secret, but I couldn't pin him down on anything.

Then my folks came. You know they finally found a nice apartment here. They smiled too when I told them how really good I felt. I know the doctors have been torturing me with so many treatments. Perhaps they have found something new that will completely cure me. There have been many miracles here in these cases before, you know.

I would have tried writing this myself, but as I said, my right hand feels weak, and I never could get my left hand to write legibly. Pearl says she has nothing better to do anyhow.

We had Thanksgiving dinner right here in the hospital. It was one of the best I've ever had. Some people here said it would be a rotten thing to be in the hospital during the holidays, but I'm finding it to be just the opposite. They've sent a lot of patients home, so we get extra attention because there are fewer of us.

I feel kind of sorry for some of those that they did send home. Some of them are being sent back home because there just isn't anymore the hospital staff can do for them, and so they go home to die. Although, I guess that would really be the best place to be—when it's your time.

Anyhow, on to more cheerful things. I'm so happy things seem to be looking up for your mom and dad. I feel I know your father. Remember when you first told me about him and how he loved to appear in your community theater? I loved your telling about Paint Your Wagon *and how he named you after one of the songs.*

Mariah, I do not want you to visit me here. I would really rather have you wait until I am better—which I am getting. I want to at least gain back a few pounds and grow some of the hair I've lost. I want to see you in an old familiar place—like my house —or maybe I could come to your home and meet your father and sit with you on your rock. After all, I shared mine with you.

I love you,
Faithfully,
Paul

Dear Paul,

I miss you terribly, Paul. I'm a little hurt that you don't want me to come and visit you in Texas, but if this is the way you want it, then that's the way it will be. Anyhow you might be home before you know it, and I'll drive to Palm Springs to visit.

Dad spent Thanksgiving with us.

It was wonderful, like we were a whole family, again. I just know in my heart that things at the Johnson house will be just like they used to be. I just know it!

My mother says she is getting me the perfect gift for Christmas, and I can hardly wait. But you know, Paul, the perfect gift would be to have you well again.

I love you,
Mariah

Chapter 27

There are no white Christmases in the southern part of California. Oh, there's usually some snow up in the mountains by December, and you can see the white-capped peaks while surfing in our ocean. But I've always wanted to wake up some Christmas morning and see that it had snowed, truly snowed, right on my windowsill.

Christmas eve we all went to the church up on the hill. My mother held my father's hand while we sang the carols. It was as though the two years my father had been away never existed. I just know that everything will eventually be okay with them and that the past will seem like a closed chapter in a book you know you'll never read again.

Christmas morning my mother placed a huge box before me. "Be careful, it's fragile!"

At first I thought it was a joke and Kim jumped up and down in her excitement. "I know what it is. I know what it is!" she squealed.

"Congratulations, honey," my mother said to her. "I never thought you'd be able to keep this secret!"

My mother lifted the smaller box inside the big box out for me and placed it on the dining room table. The label on the box gave it away! A typewriter! I couldn't believe it! A portable-electric!

My mother smiled broadly. "Oh, Mom, I don't believe it! You're terrific," I said, hugging her. She then bent over and helped me pull out the huge staples in the box. Inside was a brown suitcase. I flipped the latch open—and there it was. Lovingly I stroked the keys, and the smell of its newness filled my nose like perfume.

"I hope you like this one," she said, touching my hair. "If you'd rather have a different brand, I'll exchange it for another."

"Don't you dare touch it," I told her, covering the machine with my body. "I love it. I wouldn't dream of exchanging it!"

Taking two stairs at a time, I raced with the typewriter to my bedroom. My desk was really beginning to look like a writer's. My dictionary, *Roget's Thesaurus*, a few writer's magazines I had picked up in a bookstore in Laguna Beach, and a thick stack of blank white paper just waiting to be used. And now, to complete the picture, a real typewriter.

I slid one of the white sheets into the machine and plugged it in. And then I typed, *Dear Paul*, I began. I wrote and wrote and the typewriter softly hummed.

I didn't even hear the phone ring as I slipped out of the house. There was a mailbox right at the top of the hill and I wanted to mail my letter to Paul as quickly as I could.

The last piece of mail I'd received from him

was a Christmas card that I had propped up on my chest of drawers so that I could see it first thing each morning. It wasn't a letter—not even a small note—just a Christmas card. Paul had written only three words on it and then he had signed his name. I could hardly recognize his handwriting—it looked like an old man's.

On the card was a picture of tall evergreens standing deep in white snowdrifts. Tiny birds were trimming the trees, holding gold and silver ribbons in their beaks.

The printing inside of it said, "Love to you on this special of all days." Then down below Paul had written his three words: *Sometimes, remember me....* and then he had signed his full name.

"Oh, I wish Paul could be here right now and see that typewriter," I said out loud to the sea gulls who were already forming their little classes on the sand. I climbed up my rock and stood at the very top, looking out to the ocean. It was a cool, brisk, clear day and it had been a good Christmas so far.

I looked up at the house and saw my mother coming out the side door. At first I thought she was headed for the car, maybe running back to the store for something she needed for dinner. But, no, she was heading down the hill and then straight for me. She looked like she'd been crying.

"Hi," I called out cheerfully. "I'll let you join me on the rock if you want."

"Mariah," she said, scrambling up to me. "I want to talk to you."

We both sat down side by side, and the wind swirled my hair into my eyes. The wind was cool, but the sun still shone brightly. The beach was deserted; most people were still at home opening their gifts, playing with new toys, having fun with all the new computer games out this year.

"You look sad," I told her. And then I reached out my hand. "Is everything okay?" I asked, a tremor in my voice. Suddenly I knew something was terribly wrong.

"It's Paul," my mother said. "Mariah, I wish to God I didn't have to be the one to tell you. Mr. Strobe called when you left to mail your letter. Paul died . . . early this morning. He died at home in his own house, in Palm Springs."

He'd died while I was still asleep, I thought. While I was still dreaming of a beautiful Christmas day ahead of me. He'd died and I'd never even felt him leave. They had sent him home for Christmas. He'd been one of the patients they had sent home because there just wasn't any more they could do. . . .

I thought of his card. I hadn't thought to look at the postmark on the envelope or his return address. Of course, it had been sent from his home. And the words he had written. "Sometimes, remember me." He had told me that day on the mountain that you can keep someone alive forever by just remembering them once in a while. He was asking me to do that for him. I'll never forget you, Paul, I vowed.

The wind tore at my hair again; I gasped

and drew in the sharpness of it. I looked up at my mother as though she was not real. I was just imagining the whole thing. She put her arm around me and drew me close. My eyes stayed wide open. I knew if I were to start to cry, it would never stop.

Chapter 28

A faint sound of Christmas carols drifted up the stairs and under my closed bedroom door. I lay in the bleak darkness, holding my breath until I had to gasp for air, and then I held my breath again. Holding my mouth very rigid, I could control myself. I still would not cry.

A streak of light grew wide from out in the hall and my mother opened my bedroom door. "Are you awake?" she asked foolishly, and then she bent over me and brushed my hair from my face.

"You shouldn't stay up here alone, Mariah."

"I don't want to talk to you," I told her, burying my face further into the pillow.

"I understand," my mother said. "But I want to talk to you—and I will." I pulled the blanket halfway over my head, but I could still hear her.

"I want you to think now of the others who are suffering," she went on. "I want you to think of Paul's mother and father. This is the greatest loss of their lives. Their only consolation now is the realization that at one time they thought they could never have a child. Instead, God gave them a child and he allowed them to keep that child for all of eighteen beautiful years. How much better to have had those eighteen years than nothing at all."

We sat in the darkness. I thought of Mrs. Strobe. She had tried so hard to protect her son, to keep him from his illness. And Mr. Strobe who had tried so hard to smile through it all, to be gracious, to welcome me into the short time he had to share with Paul.

"And I want you to think of Paul. Yes, Paul," she went on. "He would have hated to see you here, hiding in the dark. He loved life so much, so very much. Don't make him disappointed in you now."

I thought of Paul and my mouth began to relax as I thought of him—his sandy hair, his wonderful smile, his eyes so blue like a summer sky, the way he'd held me that day on his rock.

My eyes grew moist, remembering. The tears squeezed out the sides of my eyes and then they were tumbling finally over my cheeks. I sat up in bed and looked at my mother, barely being able to see her through the tears. "Oh, Mom," I cried, "I will miss him so...."

She reached out and folded me into her arms. "Mom, why couldn't my story, my real life story have a happy ending—like in the books?" Finally the tears were coming, a waterfall of grief I had kept in.

"No true love story has a happy ending," she said gently, stroking my hair. "One always must die and leave the other. So there's never a totally happy ending. It's good you're finally crying now, Mariah. We must cry, you know.

But the tears are for yourself. You're crying now for your own loss. Now go and do something for Paul. Paul passed through your life for a good reason. Now go and find it, Mariah; I know you can do it."

Chapter 29

The morning of January the second, Amy knocked on our kitchen door. "Hi," she called. "Did you have a nice Christmas? Did you miss me?" She didn't know about Paul and something told me now was not the right time to tell her.

I opened the screen door and let her in. "Amy, I didn't think you'd be home from Pasadena today. I thought you said the fourth—"

"Mom's expecting company from the East," she told me, grabbing a big red Roman apple from the kitchen table. "Do you mind? I'm trying to stick to fruit instead of doughnuts now."

"Sure," I told her. "What did you get for Christmas?"

"New clothes, mostly," she said in between crunching the apple. "And I've got to keep my weight down or I won't be able to wear them." She laughed. "And how about you?"

"The best present in the world," I told her. "Come on upstairs, and I'll show you."

Amy saw it the second she entered my bedroom. "Oh, Mariah!" she exclaimed. "I love it. I love it!" She touched the smooth keys, stepped back, and touched the keys again. "Mariah, you're so lucky!"

I smiled. "Yes," I agreed. "It is something I always dreamed of having."

Amy hadn't been in my bedroom since the summer. She went over to my vanity table and poked at her hair and then she saw it. "What's that bumper sticker doing on your mirror?" she asked, pointing at the yellow strip.

"I know, it's pretty corny," I told her, "but Paul wanted me to put it up somewhere where I could see it every day. And that's where it stays."

Amy moved back to my typewriter again. "You're starting, you're actually starting to write!" she exclaimed, bending over to read what was in the machine. I had just finished typing the title when she'd appeared at the kitchen door. She read it off slowly, "P.S. I Love You." She laughed. "Oh, how cute. Palm Springs, I Love You. Can I read it?"

"When it's finished," I said.

She grabbed her sweater then. "Well, I've got to go now, Mariah, or my mom will kill me! I promised I'd only stay a few minutes. I have to go and help her with the house."

I walked downstairs with her and waved as she ran down the hill. Then I slowly closed the screen door. Amy didn't have to know that the title really meant, Paul Strobe, I Love You. It would be my secret—and Paul's—forever.

You'll fall in love with all the Sweet Dream romances. Reading these stories, you'll be reminded of yourself or of someone you know. There's Jennie, the *California Girl*, who becomes an outsider when her family moves to Texas. And Cindy, the *Little Sister*, who's afraid that Christine, the oldest in the family, will steal her new boyfriend. Don't miss any of the Sweet Dreams romances.

☐ 22683	SECRET IDENTITY #22 Joanna Campbell	$1.95
☐ 22840	FALLING IN LOVE AGAIN #23 Barbara Conklin	$1.95
☐ 22957	THE TROUBLE WITH CHARLIE #24 Jaye Ellen	$1.95
☐ 22543	HER SECRET SELF #25 Rhondi Villot	$1.95
☐ 22692	IT MUST BE MAGIC #26 Marian Woodruff	$1.95
☐ 22681	TOO YOUNG FOR LOVE #27 Gailanne Maravel	$1.95
☐ 23053	TRUSTING HEARTS #28 Jocelyn Saal	$1.95
☐ 23101	NEVER LOVE A COWBOY #29 Jesse Dukore	$1.95
☐ 23102	LITTLE WHITE LIES #30 Lois I. Fisher	$1.95
☐ 23189	TOO CLOSE FOR COMFORT #31 Debra Spector	$1.95
☐ 23190	DAYDREAMER #32 Janet Quin-Harkin	$1.95
☐ 23283	DEAR AMANDA #33 Rosemary Vernon	$1.95
☐ 23287	COUNTRY GIRL #34 Melinda Pollowitz	$1.95
☐ 23338	FORBIDDEN LOVE #35 Marian Woodruff	$1.95
☐ 23339	SUMMER DREAMS #36 Barbara Conklin	$1.95
☐ 17846	PORTRAIT OF LOVE #37 Jeanette Noble	$1.95
☐ 17847	RUNNING MATES #38 Jocelyn Saal	$1.95
☐ 23509	FIRST LOVE #39 Debra Spector	$1.95
☐ 23510	SECRETS #40 Anna Aaron	$1.95
☐ 23531	THE TRUTH ABOUT ME AND BOBBY V. #41 Janetta Johns	$1.95
☐ 23532	THE PERFECT MATCH #42 Marian Woodruff	$1.95

Prices and availability subject to change without notice.